Out of the Darkness

M. Mitchell

Out of the Darkness

Malcolm Mitchell

ATHENA PRESS
LONDON

ISBN: 978 1 84748 392 8

First published 2008 by
ATHENA PRESS
Queen's House, 2 Holly Road
Twickenham TW1 4EG
United Kingdom

Printed for Athena Press

This book is dedicated to my pilot,
Ray Isaacson, an Australian,
and to the rest of my crew.
Without their courage and professionalism,
this book may never have been written.

Acknowledgements

I am vastly indebted to Mr Tony Mawby, whose meticulous expertise in researching the background of 190 and 644 squadron's history at the military archive based at Kew, near London, has infinitely improved upon my own recollections of that war period, 1943–46.

Following Tony's sudden and tragic death while engaged upon this research, I would also like to thank his brother, 'Pip' Mawby, for sorting out Tony's work and delivering it into my hands again, having extricated it from the rest of Tony's manifold other topics.

Author Biography

My mother, Miss Ada May, married Mr Harold Mitchell in October 1915. He was a member of the Royal Air Corps at this time. In April 1916 a son, Albert (named after his uncle Albert, a soldier, killed in 1915) was born. He lived for two years, then died from meningitis. A second son, George, was born in January 1918. Later, I was conceived, but, sadly, my father succumbed to the fatal influenza which was plaguing Europe at that time. My mother was then forced to put George into an Ex Serviceman's orphanage, and seek work as a chambermaid, which she found in a London hotel until the time came for her to enter the Salvation Army's maternity hospital to give birth to me, Malcolm Mitchell. Her aunt then offered a home to us both in Acton, Middlesex. After obtaining employment as a barmaid, May, as she preferred to be called, met and married Mr Edgar Thomas, leaving me with my great aunt. The newlyweds were able to rent a flat in Acton. In August 1924, they had a son, Edwin, and finally they found a house and were able to bring me to join my mother's new family. Edwin and I became brothers, despite our different fathers.

I had a happy childhood, but economic circumstances forced me to leave school at fourteen. I joined my stepfather at D Napier and Sons, an aero engine manufacturer, first as an errand 'boy' and then, as I grew older, being reallocated to the fitting department, to be trained as a fitter assembler.

In 1942 I joined the Air Training Corps as a ground fitter, but at that stage of the war, the RAF's bomber fleet were suffering horrific losses and I was offered the option of retraining as an aircrew Flight Engineer, which I happily accepted. Then, in 1943, I visited the RAF's London headquarters, and, after an oral and written examination, was accepted for the RAF. My time in the Air Force is dealt with in this book, so I now jump to my post-war life, picking up where the book leaves off.

Leaving the post of technical author, I obtained work as a toolmaker's mate. After six months I was offered the post of Temporary Teacher in an Acton school, which I accepted as a good grounding for my future career. After a year there, I was offered a place at the Shoreditch Teacher Training College. Two years later, I won a Diploma course at the Sheffield Training College, after which I obtained temporary work until the autumn start of a teaching post with the London County Council, the LCC (now Greater London Council, or GLC). I retired early in 1970, for health reasons, after which I held various jobs, including the Civil Service, until I finished paid work in 1981. I then undertook voluntary work with Unified Community Action, which seeks to give advice, office help, etc, to the manifold voluntary organisations – religious, social, and others – in Acton.

In my social life I have been a Secretary of two Community Associations, mainly the East Acton Association, a School Governor, and a Trustee to the Acton (Middlesex) Church Charities. In my political life I have been a candidate for office on the Acton, and later, the Greater London Borough of Ealing: Candidate for the Greater London Council, and a Parliamentary Prospective Candidate for the Acton Consistency. But, as a member of a minority party, I have never been elected to these Authorities!

In 1993 I retired from Acton to Dunstable, where I founded a Pensioner's Association, of which I am still the Chairman. In my union work I moved from Ealing National Union of Teachers to the Dunstable and Luton NUT, of which I have been President. As the union's Trades Union Delegate, I joined the Luton branch, if which I am now President.

I now list my family. The birth of Steven, my eldest, is in the book itself. Moira followed in August 1947, Ruth in January 1951, and Malcolm Jnr in 1958. Sadly, my daughter Moira has passed away, but the others are well and fit. I have five grandchildren and five great-grandchildren as well. This September, my wife and I will celebrate sixty-three years of very happily married life.

Not a bad record for an eight-five-year-old!

MALCOLM MITCHELL

Some Relevant Dates

1942

1 October – Joined Air Training Corps

1943

15 May – Joined Royal Air Force

12 June – Went to Torquay

5 August – Went to St Athans

1944

25 January – Became qualified flight engineer

5 February – Went to Tilstock

4 April – Went to Fairford

28 April – First operation

11 April – F E Mitchell, a fellow flight engineer, killed on take-off*

6 June – D-Day

20 June – On leave at Acton; had V-1 raid

17 September – Arnhem operation commenced

9 October — Trip to Italy

9 October – First Norway operation

15 December – Christmas; aborted food drop. Served 'Erk's' dinner

---

* He was no relative of mine, but his death came as a distinct shock to me as I realised that it could easily have been a report of my own demise.

1945

7 February – Bombed Germany

24 March – Rhine crossing operation

31 March – Met Elizabeth at Sarratt

18 April – Repatriating British POWs from Brussels

8 May – VE day

10 May – Norway Liberation Operation

28 June – Posted from 190 Squadron to Weathersfield

9 July – Met new crew

15 August – VJ day

3 September – Got married

29 November – Went to Palestine

1946

25 February – Qastina attacked

3 March – To Bilbeis, Egypt

17 April – Return to Qastina

28 June – Son born

20 September – To Almaza, Egypt

19 November – Left Egypt

18 November – Back to England

30 November – Demobbed

Contents

Early Days

Born in October of 1922, I was raised in the West London Borough of Acton. During this period (the 1920s and '30s), Acton was held to be the largest area of light industry south of Coventry, and was home to firms such as D Napier & Son, makers of motor vehicles and aeroplane engines; Wilkinson Sword, producing garden tools and razor blades; Lucas Ltd, makers of electrical equipment for motor vehicles; CA Vandervel (CAV), electricians and motor ignition specialists, and many other industrial concerns. Acton was also home to well over one hundred laundries, causing the area to be known far and wide as 'Soapsuds Island'.

In 1936, at the age of fourteen, I completed my formal education and left school. My stepfather was on the clerical staff at Napiers, and he put in a word for me. I was duly taken on at 'Naps' as a 'boy' in an inspection department, with the job of fetching tools from the stores in the machine shop when required. In due course, I was transferred to a department making oil coolers for aero engines, where I became a trainee fitter/assembler. By this time, Napier had long since ceased to produce motor vehicles, but was still making aero engines and also engines for the high-speed motor launches of the Royal Navy and Royal Air Force.

In 1940, when I was eighteen, I moved on to Ultra Electric Ltd, another Acton firm, which was subcontracting for the aircraft makers Short Bros of Rochester, Kent. Ultra was making rudders, elevators, bomb doors, instrument panels and other parts for the new four-engined Short Stirling bomber, then entering service with the Royal Air Force. My own small part in this work was to make a small fuel-port cover for this aircraft. As an aircraft worker I became subject to the Essential Works Order, under which I could not be called up for military service.

At this time, the Battle of Britain was in full swing, but after suffering heavy losses, the mass daylight raids by the German Luftwaffe were now giving way to the night Blitz, during which many cities and towns were badly damaged, with many thousands of people killed and injured. London alone was attacked on fifty-seven consecutive nights. The daylight raids continued, but on a diminishing scale.

When the German bombing of Britain began, in June 1940, the factories stopped working at first and sent their workers to the air-raid shelters as soon as the sirens were sounded. However, many of these alerts were false alarms and frequently of long duration, which disrupted war production unnecessarily. Thus, the factories continued working through the alerts until watchers on the factory roof warned of imminent danger, whereupon everyone took shelter.

On 30 September 1940 – it was a Monday – we were in the canteen eating our dinner (called lunch nowadays) when the watchers on the roof sounded the alarm, just as I was starting on a rice pudding! With plate and spoon in hand, I was walking across the yard to the shelter when I heard the sound of aero engines. Looking up, I saw six German bombers overhead, in the act of releasing their bombs!

Mercifully for us, the bombs fell on the far side of the Central Line of the London Underground, which passed close by our factory. I sped to the shelter, where I ate my pudding in comparative safety, completely unaware of the tragedy unfolding down the road.

It appears that the German bombers, possibly Junkers Ju 88s, were aiming for the fighter airfield at Northolt, which so far had hardly been touched. However, they bombed well short of the airfield and their bombs fell on a residential area of Greenford, with devastating results. More than 400 houses were destroyed and damaged, killing thirty-seven people and injuring many more. All of Northolt's fighters (Nos. 229, 1 [Canadian] and 303 [Polish] Squadrons) had been scrambled some forty minutes before and were now engaged over Kent.

As remarked earlier, being an aircraft worker I was exempt from being called up for military service. However, as I was now eighteen I was liable for some form of national service and I became a part-time fire-watcher. So far as I was concerned, this involved losing a night's sleep every Tuesday, when I would report to the fire-watching centre nearest to my home and then, with other watchers, wait for the onset of an air raid. When the sirens sounded the alarm, we patrolled in pairs, on the lookout for fires, and we were to call the fire brigade if one was found. I only once encountered an incendiary bomb but, as it was harmlessly burning itself out near a brick wall, I took no action.

In addition to the bombs and collapsing buildings, another danger, and one rarely mentioned, was that of falling shell splinters. These were the product of anti-aircraft shells, which were set to burst at predetermined heights. After being scattered by the shell burst, the splinters fell back to earth, and for anyone unfortunate enough to be in the way they could be as lethal as any bullet.

I was returning home one evening from a visit to the cinema when an air raid started, and the local ack-ack (anti-aircraft) gun battery, sited on Gunnersbury Park, was quickly in full voice. Having, on a previous outing, been near-missed by a bomb exploding in a nearby road, I was now treated to a shower of shell splinters, which bounced about on the road and the pavement, luckily without hitting me.

My link with the RAF began when I joined the Air Training Corps (ATC), becoming part of No. 263 Squadron, which met at Acton Technical College. The ATC was to train me as a ground engineer, for which I received a good grounding in maths and a thorough understanding of aeroplane engines, the main teaching aid here being a Napier Lion aero engine. At some stage, as prospective ground crew we were invited to re-muster as flight engineers. This was partly to replace casualties but mainly, as I later realised, to aid in the expansion of the heavy bomber force (Stirlings, Halifaxes and Lancasters), which required large numbers of flight engineers. I immediately accepted this offer despite the Essential Works Order, which not only barred me from being called up but also prevented me leaving Ultra Electric by choice. This problem was to be solved in an unexpected way.
Early in 1943 a works dispute – not a strike – had broken out at

Ultra over a working practice. Matters came to a head when the workforce, led by the shop stewards, marched to the office of the managing director. As I was the youth representative on the works committee, I was instructed to march at the front with the shop stewards. The managing director was not in the best of tempers when we arrived at his office, and an angry argument followed. In the middle of this, he turned his attention to me, the youngest one there and not called up, and shouted, 'Do you want to go in the f—— army?'

Unknown to him, I was already training for the RAF and I quickly replied, 'I don't give a s—!' Within a week I dismissed as 'Surplus to production needs' and freed of the Essential Works Order, enabling me to join the RAF.

Myself in the Air Training Corps, 1942.

The Royal Air Force

After my departure from Ultra Electric I lost no time in making my application to join the RAF, and I was summoned to attend an interview at Adastral House, in Kingsway, London. I was given a thorough medical examination, after which I sat written and oral examinations. One question in the written exam partially beat me by asking for the square root of sixteen. I had no idea what the symbol for square root meant! However, my paper was marked, and then one of the oral examiners asked me, 'What is the square root of sixteen?' I easily knew it to be four, passed with flying colours and was accepted for training as a flight engineer.

A few days later, I was instructed to report to an hotel in Maida Vale, which served as an annex to the RAF reception centre at the nearby Lord's Cricket Ground. The first few weeks of my RAF service were spent here, being kitted out, having inoculations, learning how to make a bed the RAF way, learning how to salute superiors and so forth. As I lived in the London area in Acton, I was allowed to go home each evening between 5 and 10 p.m., thus making my break from home and my parents' break from me more gradual and easier.

On 12 June 1943, I was posted to No. 21 Initial Training Wing located at Torquay in Devon, for a six-week introductory course for aircrew. I was given some weapons training covering the Lee Enfield rifle, Sten gun, revolver and hand grenade. I also learned Morse code (on the Aldis lamp), aircraft recognition, marching and a few other skills, all of this being punctuated by spells of physical training. Dinghy drill was undertaken in the local swimming baths, where I suffered an injury to my back which has plagued me ever since. It was a lovely summer and we all became fit as fleas.

My next move, after a fortnight's leave at home, was to MoD School of Technical Training (STT) at St Athan, near Cardiff. This was a large permanent station which had wonderful sports facilities,

Myself (right) on the seafront at Torquay with a friend. The white flash on our caps indicates we have been accepted for aircrew training.

including an Olympic-style swimming pool and large gymnasium halls.

At St Athan I received extremely thorough training in air-frames and the type of engine I was to be in charge of. I was given the choice of studying either a liquid-cooled in-line engine or an air-cooled radial type. I chose the latter as I thought that it would be more robust. After a short course on in-line engines, I found myself learning about the Bristol Hercules air-cooled sleeve-valved engine. With hindsight, I now realise that the training was excellent for ground crew, but not for a flight engineer working in the air, where a different type of knowledge would have been more useful. I had to gain that knowledge the hard way – in action.

I had to spend Christmas of 1943 in Wales, but fortunately I had an invite to have Christmas dinner with a black Welsh family, whose daughter and son I had met when I joined the Cardiff Young Communist League, the membership of which was mainly girls as the lads had mostly been called up. The daughter, a nurse, had to spend the day at her hospital, while I enjoyed a Christmas dinner in her place!

It was a regular thing for us RAF men to visit Cardiff for leisure and pleasure. One evening, returning to camp by train, several of us found ourselves in a compartment with a WAAF and two American soldiers, very tough-looking individuals. During the journey, one of them left his seat and went over to accost the girl, who was sitting opposite me. It was obvious that she did not want his advances, so I pulled the back of his greatcoat and asked him to leave her alone. 'Don't toucha da coat!' he turned round to say to me. He then turned back to resume his advances, so I grabbed his coat again and told him to let the girl be. The situation was now becoming quite ugly, but there were other RAF men in the compartment and his companion made no move to back him, so he sulkily went back to his seat, to my profound relief. He was a really big bruiser!

'B' Flight, No. 3 Squadron, 21 Initial Training Wing, Torquay, July 1943. I am on the extreme left, third row.

Qualified as a flight engineer, January 1944.

A Non-commissioned Officer

I need not have worried about passing the exams at the end of the five-month course, for I never heard of anyone who failed. One man did opt out, however, and he was transferred to ground duties, but the rest of us all passed and I received my flight engineer's brevet and the sergeant's stripes that came with it.

As a sergeant, I now had access to that most exclusive of establishments, the Sergeants' Mess, territory even more exclusive than that of the Officers' Mess, which is saying a great deal. It is not commonly known that when he is off duty, even a marshal of the Royal Air Force cannot enter the Sergeants' Mess unless invited to by the mess members. Even if on duty, no air marshal would think of entering the mess without first consulting the all-powerful Chairman of the Mess Committee, a man not to be trifled with. On perhaps a more practical level, my promotion also meant that I now enjoyed a higher rate of pay, the coins of which jingled merrily in my pocket.

My training at St Athan completed, I was sent on a three-week manufacturers' course at Marston Green, near Birmingham, where I had my first meeting with the aircraft I was to fly on operations, the Short Stirling. At this time – early 1944 – Austin Motors were building Stirlings at their Longbridge plant, sending the component parts – fuselage, wings, tailplane etc. – to Marston Green for final assembly and painting. The completed aircraft were towed to the adjoining Elmdon aerodrome (now Birmingham Airport) for flight testing, after which they were delivered to service.

My first impression of the Stirling, when seen on the ground from close up, was of its size: it was huge! Positioned on top of the fuselage, the cockpit was almost twenty-three feet above the ground. The long fuselage gave the aircraft a gaunt appearance, but the most striking feature was the undercarriage, which has been compared to scaffolding. This was a very tall and complicated affair, which was raised and lowered by two operations. When being raised, the upper part of the assembly swung forwards and upwards while the lower part hinged backwards and upwards into its housing in the wing. This assembly was vulnerable to strong side-loadings. A violent swing on take-off or landing could, and often did, cause the undercarriage to collapse, and many Stirlings were written off in this fashion.

I spent the next three weeks familiarising myself with the Stirling, particularly the fuselage. I quickly discovered that the flight engineer's seat had been removed in order not to impede a rapid evacuation, should one become necessary. Instead, I would have to sit on a metal bar which ran across the fuselage, not the most comfortable form of seating for a flight lasting eight hours or longer! My crew station was dominated by the instrument panel, which monitored engine conditions, the fuel tanks, fuel pressures, oil pressures and temperatures, all of these with their warning lights. Also on the panel were the controls for the engine cowling gills. To the immediate right of the panel a hand-held fire extinguisher was located.

A few paces aft of the panel, and part of my domain, were the controls for the fuel tank cocks, the carburettor air intakes, the superchargers, cabin heating and fuel jettison valves. Also in this area were the electrical distribution panel and the winch for the trailing wireless aerial. Nearby was the gearing for manually raising or lowering the undercarriage in the event of an electrical failure.

I learned the runs of the control cables governing the ailerons, elevators and rudder, together with their associated trimming controls. The rear turret was hydraulically powered by a pump on the starboard inner engine, and the connecting piping had to be checked for leakage.

Having absorbed all of this and much more besides, I was given one week's home leave, where I swaggered about with my brevet and sergeant's stripes. All too quickly, my leave came to an end and I was posted to 1665 Heavy Conversion Unit (HCU), based at Tilstock, in Shropshire, where I arrived on 5 February 1944.

Unlike St Athan, which was a pre-war station with permanent brick-built accommodation, Tilstock was a wartime-built station (opened in August 1942), with temporary hutted accommodation. Compared with St Athan, conditions were spartan.

While waiting to be crewed up, I and the other flight engineers on my course had to attend one of the hangars every day to give a half-hearted hand in maintaining Stirlings – work which none of us really had a clue about. We were in the charge of a ground staff warrant officer, who made it perfectly clear that he had no time for reluctant aircrew! He soon proved his point. At St Athan we had had Sundays off, except for a voluntary church parade, so we thought it was quite all right not to turn up at the hangar that day. The following day (Monday) we all trooped down to work, to find that we were all on a charge for our absence on Sunday! We had to appear before an officer, who was forced to find us guilty as charged, but let us off with the lowest punishment, an admonishment. Fortunately, I was never told to appear at the hangar again, as I was given a 'cushy' job in the control tower, monitoring aircraft movements. In passing, although it was derelict, the control tower was still standing in 1980, as were the airfield's four hangars.

A week after the unpleasantness with the warrant officer, I was issued with my flying kit, after which I went to the nearby town of Whitchurch (three miles north of the airfield) to buy a reliable watch to time my air log. The following day I had my first flight since joining the RAF. During the week that followed, I was instructed by an experienced flight engineer while actually in the air. This phase ended with a five-hour cross-country flight. Then I met the men with whom I was to fly for the next fifteen months, and began to learn my duties in the air as part of a crew.

The crew was headed by a small Australian pilot, Ray Isaacson, a farmer from Parrakie, in South Australia. The navigator, Ross Vincent, was also Australian and was a banker from Perth, a friendly flying officer and older than the rest of us. At this time, he was the only officer in the crew, the rest of us being sergeants. Next in age was Ron Bradbury, our wireless operator, a quiet and reliable person. Our bomb aimer was a cheerful young lad, Bob Sutton, who became a real friend and companion to me. The crew was completed by Arthur Batten, our rear gunner, who was a real countryman and very familiar with guns.

The training consisted mainly of continual take-offs and landings by both day and night, and simulated emergencies. In the case of the latter, I remember the hard work of lowering the undercarriage by hand, entailing about seventy turns of a hand crank let into the side of the fuselage, and also all the continual entries into my log as the engine condition changed. On one flight, the instructor threw the aircraft up, down and sideways until we were all airsick! These and other experiences welded us together as an organic crew. We were then sent out on our own on a five-hour cross-country flight, myself solo as a flight engineer for the first time. Fortunately everything went well, unlike one of our later flights when the starboard inner engine went o/s (out of service) and we had to land on three engines. I must point out that the Stirlings which we were flying were, in the main, old aircraft which had been relegated from operational to training duties, and therefore not very reliable.

With the course successfully completed we were given a week's leave, after which we received our operational posting. We were posted to No. 190 Squadron, based at Fairford, Gloucestershire, where we arrived on Monday, 3 April 1944.

The Isaacson crew, 190 Squadron.
Back row: Ron Bradbury (W/Op); Arthur Batten (A/G); Ray Isaacson (Pilot).
Front row: Myself (Flt Eng); Ross Vincent (Nav); Bob Sutton (B/Aimer).

No. 190 Squadron

Commanded by Wing Commander G E Harrison, our squadron was part of No. 38 (Airborne Forces) Group. It was equipped with Stirling Mark IVs, a later version of those we had flown at Tilstock, but modified for glider towing and paratroop operations. The most noticeable 'mod' was the deletion of the nose and mid-upper gun turrets, the nose turret being replaced by a clear perspex fairing. The rear turret, with its battery of four .303 Browning machine guns, was retained. Another 'mod' was the addition of a metal horseshoe-shaped towing bridle, which was fitted on the lower fuselage aft of the tailplane. For paratroop operations, an exit hatch measuring 6 ft by 4 ft was let into the floor of the rear fuselage, just forward of the crew entry door. This hatch could also be used for dropping supply panniers and packages. The squadron was also tasked (as were the other squadrons of 38 Group) with dropping arms and supplies to the resistance groups in enemy-occupied Europe, a duty it performed until the end of the war. These operations were carried out at night, usually during the moon period of each month.

Newly formed, 190 Squadron had arrived at Fairford only a few days before ourselves, having been formed at Leicester East on 5 January. Being only the second squadron to equip with Stirling IVs, it received most of its aircraft direct from the makers, Short & Harland Ltd, of Belfast. Glider-towing exercises began in March, and these were flown with increasing frequency as the month progressed. The gliders assisted greatly when the squadron moved to Fairford, on 25 March, by carrying equipment and other stores and generally acting as flying removal vans.

At this time, squadron personnel including attachments numbered 779, being made up with: 55 officers (air/ground crew); 133 NCOs (aircrew); 27 NCOs (ground crew); 276 airmen; 17 WAAFs; 5 NCOs and 33 airmen (Heavy Glider Servicing Unit);

80 glider pilots ('G' Squadron, Glider Pilot Regiment); 6 naval petty officers and 147 ratings. The naval personnel were Fleet Air Arm engine fitters, attached to gain experience of radial engines before being drafted to the Far East.

190 Squadron shared Fairford with the similarly equipped and tasked 620 Squadron, commanded by Wing Commander D H Lee. Both squadron commanders were to be shot down at Arnhem.

Opened the previous January, Fairford airfield was sited two miles south of Fairford town and nine miles north of Swindon. It was a typical airfield of the period, with three runways laid out in the shape of the letter 'A'. The main runway was aligned in the direction of the prevailing wind and was 6,000 ft long. The other two runways were each 4,200 ft long, and all three runways were 150 ft wide. They were connected to the aircraft dispersal points by a perimeter taxiing track, which was 50 ft wide.

As on any airfield, the hangars were a prominent feature. At Fairford, these were two prefabricated steel structures, covered by corrugated metal sheeting. They were 240 ft long with an overall width of 115 ft. The entrance was 113 ft wide by 29 ft high. The sloping roof gave a maximum height of 39 ft. This type of hangar was officially known as the T2 transportable shed.

The control tower, the nerve centre of the airfield, was a concrete building two storeys high with a flat roof which could be reached by an interior stairway. To ease blacking-out problems, the windows were small. In July of 1985, I returned to Fairford in order to attend the International Air Tattoo, which was being held there that year. The control tower was still standing and fully functional, albeit with the post-war addition of a Visual Control Room on the roof of the building, which gave the controller an all-round view of the airfield.

As with all wartime-built airfields, the station buildings (station headquarters, flight offices, briefing room, stores and billets etc.) were of a temporary nature, being prefabricated wooden and metal huts of various sizes.

The origins of Fairford town go back to at least AD 862, when it was known as 'Fagranforda'. It appears in the Domesday Book as 'Fareforda', being noted as 'King's land with three mills'. In

1944, Fairford was a lovely little country town, but with very little in the way of amusements. However, there was a frequent bus service to Swindon, a large town with cinemas, dance halls and other amenities. I spent a lot of time there and, joining the Swindon branch of the Young Communist League, made many friends.

Later, when we had been issued with bicycles to get around the large station and to get out, Bob and I cycled to many dances in Cirencester, a good distance away.

Our first action on arrival at RAF Station Fairford was to report to the orderly room. Here, we were each given a form to fill in, which asked for details of next of kin, disposal of personal effects, our assets and last wishes. This was to help the admin staff, should we fail to return from operations or be killed in an accident. We were told our hut number, where to find it, and to report back the next day.

The following morning we started the procedure of 'arrival'. This involved going around the station with our arrival chits, which had to be signed by all of the well-dispersed sections. Not yet issued with bicycles we carried out this procedure on foot, learning Fairford's layout as we went along.

Having duly arrived, we were absorbed into our squadron, being assigned to 'B' Flight, which was commanded by Squadron Leader D S Gibb, a New Zealander. The following three weeks saw our crew involved with day and night training exercises covering cross-countries, navigational exercises, glider towing, practise container dropping and target practise on the range, where Arthur honed his skills with his machine guns. At intervals, Horsa gliders were collected from the storage unit at Brize Norton, Oxfordshire. 190 Squadron had become operational at the end of March, and was now dropping supplies to the French Resistance groups. At this time, these operations were mounted from the forward airfield of Tarrant Rushton, in Dorset.

I had not been long at Fairford when the squadron suffered its first casualties. Soon after taking off from Tarrant Rushton for a supply drop in France, one of our Stirlings crashed at Hampreston, in Dorset. All of the crew were killed and the flight engineer's name was Mitchell! This was a sad and disturbing start to my time with the squadron. A few days later, a Horsa glider making a night landing at Fairford crashed into the control tower, killing the pilot.

Towards the end of April our crew was declared operational, and we awaited our first foray over enemy territory.

No. 190 Squadron badge – a cloak charged with a double-headed eagle displayed.

Motto: Ex Tenebris ('Through darkness')

Authority: King George VI, February 1945

Origin: The dark cloak refers to the squadron's role of dropping arms and supplies to the resistance groups in enemy-occupied Europe. These operations were cloaked in secrecy and always carried out at night, a point emphasised by the motto. The double-headed eagle appears in the Civic Coat of Arms of the Dutch city of Arnhem and symbolises the squadron's operations over that city and the heavy losses suffered there.

Photograph courtesy of the Imperial War Museum, London

'B' Flight, 190 Squadron, June 1944
Second row: far left, Ross Vincent; second left, Ron Bradbury, third left, Arthur Batten. Third row: third left, Ray Isaacson; fourth left, myself; fifth left, Bob Sutton.

The First Operation

In the morning of 28 April, our crew appeared on the squadron's battle order for the first time. That afternoon, with three other squadron crews, we flew to Tarrant Rushton, from where the operation was to be mounted. We were briefed for a supply flight deep into France, to a drop zone (DZ) near the Swiss border. Our load consisted of twenty-four containers, carrying arms, ammunition, explosives and other supplies needed by the local Resistance group. The other three squadron crews were briefed for different drop zones and would follow their own routes.

The last to take off, we left the ground at 2310 hrs and climbed steadily to 10,000 ft, where we would be above the low-level flak. Once over the English Channel, Arthur Batten requested permission to test his guns, and this was granted. As we crossed the French coast we ran into the belt of the German coastal flak and Ikey (short for Isaacson), our pilot, put the aircraft into a series of evasive turns and changes of height to prevent the flak getting our range. As this was my first taste of enemy fire (although I had experienced being bombed during the Blitz) my feelings were mixed: partly interest in the show and partly fear that we would be hit. But the danger passed quickly and we were soon out over the quiet French countryside inland. Once clear of the coastal flak we came down to between 500 and 200 ft, and from there to the DZ (drop zone) was peaceful flying. The main reason for flying at low level was to make life difficult for the German night fighters, making it almost impossible for them to track us due to the 'ground clutter' on their radar scopes. It also enabled Bob, our bomb aimer, to look through the clear nose fairing and assist the navigator (Ross) by map reading our way to the drop zone, avoiding built-up areas and known flak positions. A radar homing beacon, Eureka, which transmitted to the Rebecca receivers in our aircraft, was available, but for various reasons was little used by the French Resistance groups.

I was always surprised at how clear the view of the ground seemed, even on nights when there was not much moon. We usually operated on nights when there was little cloud but, of course, there were exceptions. On one operation we ran into really awful weather, so bad that it stripped the paint from the side of the Stirling!

After Ross and Bob had between them navigated us across France, we arrived over a predetermined major landmark; I forget now what it was. From there, we made a timed run to our designated drop zone, which we duly reached and circled at 500 ft. On the ground, three members of the reception committee, holding torches, were strung out in a line along the direction of the wind. The leader of the committee, also holding a torch, was positioned so that the lights, as seen from the air, resembled a reversed capital 'L', which indicated the wind direction. At the sound of our approach all of the lights turned in our direction, the leader's light Morsing a prearranged letter. Our own signalling light Morsed back the appropriate countersign, at which a bonfire was lit in the chosen field. Ikey opened the bomb doors and circled us into the wind for the drop. We made our run-in, and Bob, lying at his station in the nose of the aircraft and below the flight deck, released the containers on their parachutes to the brave people waiting below, reporting, 'Containers gone.' At the same time, Arthur called from the rear turret, reporting that all parachutes had been seen to open. I had put the engines on to the main fuel tanks for these manoeuvres, and now reverted to the recommended order for the use of the various tanks in the wings.

Then it was up and away from the area of the DZ as quickly as possible, as our continued presence could endanger the people on the ground either from a German land patrol or a prowling night fighter. Once clear of the area, we settled down for the long flight home which, fortunately, was uneventful. So it was back to England, safety and daylight, landing at Tarrant Rushton at 0516 hrs. We were debriefed and our aircraft was checked and refuelled, while we ate a breakfast in the mess, after which we were free to fly back to our own base at Fairford. Of the four squadron crews over France that night, ours was the only successful sortie. The others had met with no reception at their DZs, and were forced to bring their loads back to Tarrant Rushton.

At this point it might be appropriate to describe the supply containers we carried. There were several versions, but the most commonly used was the C-type metal container. Made of strengthened sheet metal, the C-type was cylindrical in shape, 5 ft 9 in. long and 15 in. wide. It was hinged along its whole length and the two halves were held shut by three quick-release catches, which were prevented from premature opening by split pins. It could carry a load of up to 220 lbs, giving an overall weight of 330 lbs. One end of the container formed a cowling to accommodate the parachute, which deployed to a diameter of 22 ft. At the other end of the container was the impact-absorbing head. This was a metal dome with large cut-outs, designed to assist its collapse, thereby absorbing the force of the impact when the container hit the ground. Several people would be needed to carry a loaded container, and to that end four carrying handles were fitted. The Stirling could carry a maximum of twenty-four containers, (more than any other Allied aircraft), eighteen in the fuselage bomb bay and six in the wing bomb cells. In the event of a long-range operation, such as a trip to Norway, the wing cells would carry auxiliary fuel tanks instead of containers.

Another form of container frequently used was the pannier. This was made of wicker with a specially padded interior, and was the shape and size of a laundry basket. Less robust items, such as wireless sets, were carried in these. Panniers were carried in the fuselage of the aircraft and were pushed out through the exit hole in the floor by the flight engineer. The size of the parachute varied with the weight of the pannier, which could be as much as 140 lb.

Training exercises continued throughout May, but these did not pass off without incident. On 19 May, two Stirlings of 620 Squadron were returning from a glider-towing exercise when they collided at 400 ft over the rope-dropping area, on the edge of the airfield circuit. Both aircraft crashed near Kempsford, close to Fairford. There were no survivors.

As the month wore on, there were increasing signs that the long-awaited Allied invasion of Western Europe was approaching. On both sides of the country roads and lanes around Fairford, huge quantities of bombs, shells and other munitions had been stockpiled. We spent much of our free time in Swindon, and we often passed by these great piles of explosives, which were miles long and several feet high.

At the end of May, the 1st SAS Regiment arrived at Fairford and occupied a campsite adjacent to the airfield. The campsite was completely sealed off, surrounded by barbed wire and patrolled by armed sentries. The soldiers were addressed by their commanding officer, Lieutenant Colonel Blair 'Paddy' Mayne, who informed them in no uncertain terms that the only way they would leave Fairford would be in an aircraft bound for France!

The first indication that D-Day was imminent came on 31 May, when the supply flights to the French Resistance groups were suspended and flying restricted to air tests. A further indication came on 2 June, when the station was sealed off to the outside world and the ground crews began to adorn the outer wings and rear fuselages of our Stirlings with the black and white invasion stripes. Two days later, in the course of a whistle-stop tour, Air Chief Marshal Sir Trafford Leigh-Mallory (Commander-in-Chief, Allied Air Forces) visited Fairford and addressed the aircrews of 190 and 620 Squadrons. This was followed by a final flurry of air tests, and by 1800 hrs of 5 June our squadron had thirty-eight Stirlings ready to operate.

Operation Overlord

In the afternoon of 5 June, twenty-three crews (ours was not included), each of 190 and 620 Squadrons, were summoned to the briefing hut. They were briefed for Operation 'Tonga', in which elements of the British 6th Airborne Division were to be dropped on a DZ in the Ouistreham area of France. Despite the weather, which was overcast with strong winds, the operation was to take place that night. D-Day had arrived.

That evening the atmosphere in the Sergeants' Mess became electric. After the evening meal, some 6th Airborne Division lads, glider pilots and others, began drinking and generally letting off steam, a process which ended by them stacking up all of the furniture in the mess at one end of the building. They then began to clamber up this piled-up jumble to reach the metal struts holding up the roof, from which they attempted to swing! We staid RAF types could only watch in amazement.

Led by Wing Commander Harrison, our squadron's aircraft started to take off on 'Tonga' at 2315 hrs, and by 2332 hrs all were safely airborne and on their way to France. Light flak was encountered in the target area, but all of our aircraft returned safely. However, 620 Squadron was not so fortunate; three of their aircraft failed to return. One of our aircraft was unable to locate the DZ, and was forced to bring back its load of eighteen disgruntled paratroopers.

The following day, we were one of eighteen squadron crews detailed for Operation 'Mallard'. In company with eighteen crews of 620 Squadron, we were briefed to tow gliders to LZ 'W' (Landing Zone 'W'), a little to the south of Ouistreham. The gliders would be lifting reinforcements to the 6th Airborne Division, which was holding the flank of the invasion bridgehead until being relieved by ground forces advancing from 'Sword' beach. The glider our crew was to tow carried three men, a jeep, trailer and a 75 mm gun. The tug aircraft and the glider formed a

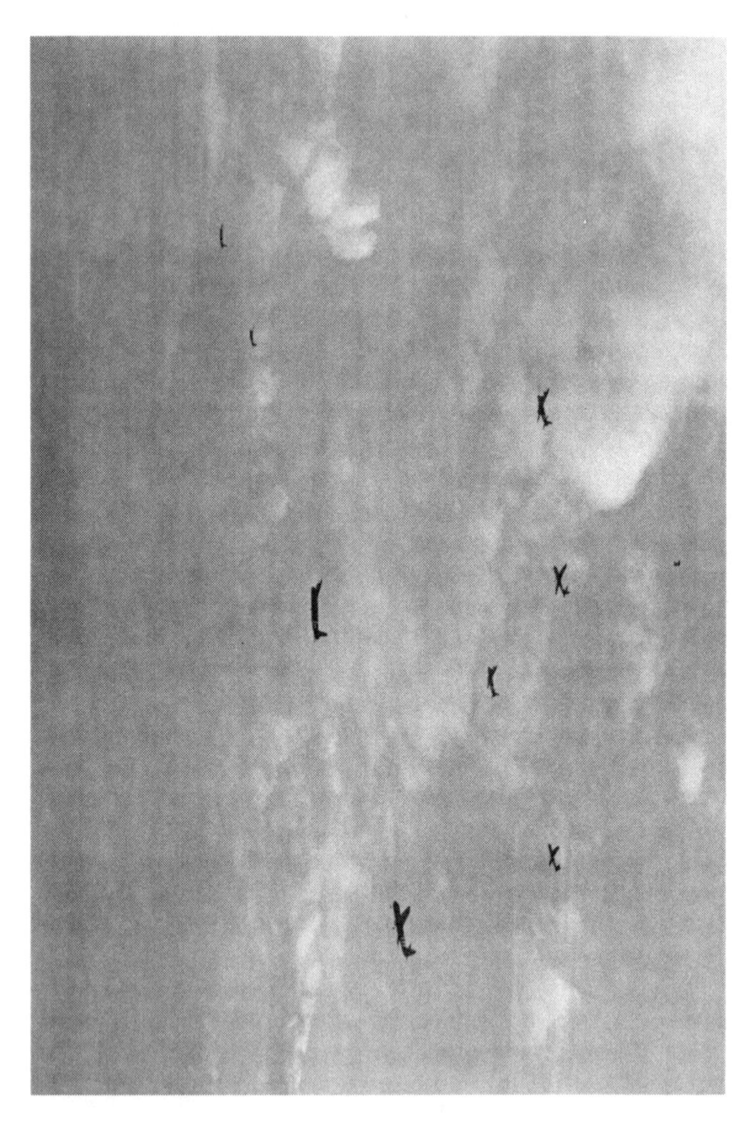

6 June 1944. Stirling/Horsa combinations en route to Normandy.
Photograph courtesy of the Imperial War Museum, London

'combination' and our crew was part of combination 215, this number being chalked on the fuselage of the glider and that of the tug.

When we came out to the airfield, finding the weather to be good and sunny, a memorable sight greeted us. Ranged along the near end of the runway were two lines of Horsa gliders, each with its tow rope connected and neatly laid out. Parked diagonally on each side of the runway, and abreast of the gliders, were our Stirlings. Units of soldiers were marching here and there while other groups, including glider pilots, stood by the gliders. To complete the scene, RAF ground crews were moving purposefully about, checking that all was ready.

We made our way to our Stirling (LJ881 Z-Zebra), where I made my pre-flight checks of the undercarriage and tyres and took a general look around, after which I joined the others inside the aircraft. I turned on the cocks for the main fuel tanks (nos. 2 and 4 in each wing), after which I turned my attention to the two-speed supercharger controls – one for each engine – checking that these were set for 'low'. Moving forward to my instrument panel, I set the engine cowling gills to one-third open, this being shown by the indicators on the panel and by a visual check through the astrodome. Meanwhile, the other crew members were looking to their own instruments and equipment – flying, navigation, bomb aiming, wireless and guns. Having completed his checks, Bob, our bomb aimer, was now sitting in the second pilot's seat, where he would assist Ikey with the take-off.

With all checks completed, Ikey signalled to the ground crew to give the starter motors of each engine in turn (port outer and inner, starboard inner and outer) the electrical charge to start the engines. As the engines coughed and then burst into life, Ikey manipulated the throttles to settle them down to a steady beat, I was now at my instrument panel, checking that all was well with the engine temperatures and oil pressure and temperatures etc.

One at a time, the Stirlings ahead of us in the line moved onto the runway, where they were linked up to their gliders and then took off. Eventually, our turn came. The chocks in front of the main wheels were pulled away and the brakes were released. We gained the runway, turned on, lined up and stopped. The wing flaps were extended to one-third out, and at the same time the glider's tow rope was attached to the towing bridle at the rear of the Stirling's fuselage. This done, we slowly moved forward a few yards to take up the slack until Arthur, who was watching from his turret, told Ikey the towrope was taut.

Holding the aircraft on the brakes, Ikey ran up the engines to 2,000 rpm, at which point Bob took over the manipulation of the throttle levers, allowing Ikey to release the brakes and apply both hands to the control column. Bob now pushed the throttle levers all the way forward, with the starboard throttles ahead of the port throttles to counteract the Stirling's tendency to swing to starboard on take-off before the rudder became effective. With the engines at take-off boost, we picked up speed and at about 70 mph the glider left the ground. Still we thundered down the runway to reach our own take-off speed of 120 mph, and we slowly lifted off the deck, becoming airborne at 1950 hrs. All this time I was by my panel, with eyes glued to the instruments to see that all was well with the engines, for take-off and landing are two periods of danger for an aircraft, and we were towing a glider, which added to the drag on our Stirling. However, all was well, as was usually the case.

As we climbed away, Bob braked the undercarriage wheels, which were still spinning, then raised the undercarriage. Once that was up and locked, he released the wheel brakes, after which he raised the wing flaps.

The glider took up a high-tow position, above the backwash from our propellers, as we climbed to our briefed height of 1,500 ft. We formatted on the Stirling ahead of us, joining an immense stream of aircraft which was circling over the English countryside to accomplish the planned formation, eventually turning to head out over the coast towards Normandy. Then came a sight never to be forgotten. There were aircraft and gliders as far as the eye could see, ahead and behind us, with fighter aircraft chaperoning us on all sides. Below, on the sea, was a seemingly endless stream of ships, all heading the same way – and not an enemy in sight!

As we neared the coast of Normandy, Bob left the second pilot's seat and went down to his position in the nose. In addition to towing the glider, we were carrying nine supply containers, which would be dropped after the glider had cast off. I went aft to wind in the trailing aerial, which had to be done before the containers were dropped, then returned to my lookout position in the astrodome, from where I could see the town of Caen to starboard and a pattern of rivers and flat coastal land ahead. We crossed the coast at 1,100 ft and our glider immediately cast off and began its descent. We continued straight and level for a few seconds, then Bob released our nine containers; all of the parachutes were seen to open. We about-turned to starboard, near Caen, then dropped the tow rope and headed back out to sea. During the period over land (just five minutes) we ourselves had encountered no flak, no opposition of any sort. However, six of our aircraft had been damaged by light flak and machine-gun fire, fatally wounding one of the bomb aimers. 620 Squadron lost one Stirling, but the crew all escaped and were back at Fairford a few days later. Of the enemy air force there was no sign. Our command of the air was absolute!

The return flight to England showed similar sights to those met with on the way out, but we now had more leisure to look at what was happening. We noted a ditched Halifax off the French coast and a motor launch heading towards it. We later heard that all of the crew were rescued. Reaching the English coast, we passed over a crowded invasion port (Portsmouth?) before turning for base, where we landed at 2340 hrs.

A few figures might be appropriate at this point. In the first twenty-four hours of 'Overlord', the Allied air forces flew a total of 14,674 sorties for the loss of 113 aircraft, mostly to flak. In the same period, as part of this effort, aircraft of 38 and 46 Groups of the RAF and the American 9th Troop Carrier Command flew a combined total of 2,292 sorties (2,187 effective), landing 24,424 troops by parachute and glider. This was additional to the 132,000 seaborne troops put ashore on the invasion beaches (Sword, Juno, Gold, Omaha and Utah).

The landings went well, from our point of view, and our crew was not required to return to the beachhead except for a supply drop near Ouistreham. Then, for us, it was back to the business of supplying the Resistance groups in enemy-occupied Europe, especially France, where they were very active indeed.

Resistance Drops Again

During the rest of June, throughout July and August and well into September, our squadron operated with increasing frequency over France, reaching a peak in August. During this period our crew flew thirteen operations, and for us these were mostly uneventful and incident free, but such was not always the case. One operation was made most memorable as it was very nearly our last!

Setting off after nightfall, as was usually the case for French operations, we crossed the Channel into France, finding that the flak belt had more or less disappeared, although we could see flak and searchlights to the west. Once inland, we came down to low level (300 to 500 ft) and set course for our briefed drop zone, which we duly reached. We exchanged the prearranged identification letters with the reception committee on the ground after which we lined up, made our run-in and dropped our load of twenty-four containers. We began to climb away, but then the aircraft suddenly tilted nose down and on my instrument panel four red lights appeared, indicating that all four engines were receiving no petrol. I at once jumped about four paces to the rear of the aircraft, where the two banks of fuel cocks were located, and threw every cock on. The aircraft then righted itself, to my relief, and the red lights disappeared.

As we then climbed away, we learned what the trouble had been. I have to tell you that we were always given a pre-flight meal of bacon and eggs (usually powdered eggs) before an operation, and understand that the manoeuvres to descend, making the run and then climbing again imposed a certain stress on the pilot. Ikey had suffered a stomach upset, and as we climbed away from the DZ he had fainted over the controls, sending the aircraft plunging from our already low altitude. Bob, who usually acted as second pilot, was still 'downstairs' at his station in the lower nose of the aircraft, and it would have gone ill with us but for an extraordinary stroke of luck. That night, an army glider pilot had asked to come on the operation with us, and he was sitting in the second pilot's seat. He had reached across, pushed Ikey away from the controls and righted the aircraft.

The four red lights which I had seen had appeared as the result of a sudden change of G (gravity) forces, which had starved all the engines of fuel. We had never been closer to a crash, the cause of which would have remained unexplained. As it was, we were able to make a safe and uneventful journey home.

Returning from another operation over France, we noticed a long train below puffing through the night. Arthur pleaded with Ikey for the chance to machine-gun it, having never had the opportunity to fire his guns in anger. We swooped down and followed up the line to allow him to strafe the train, which he did. However, we saw no satisfactory explosion of steam from the locomotive and so, reluctantly, we climbed away into the night.

The days and weeks passed and our crew's tally of operations steadily increased. As a note of our growing experience, we now sometimes had a seventh crew member assigned to us. This might be a pilot, navigator or flight engineer, or some other crew member. Nearing the end of their training at the conversion unit, these aircrew would be briefly attached to the squadron in order to gain some operational experience before going on operations with their own crews.

The operations over France proved to be well worthwhile. In addition to the SAS operations in which we were involved, those undertaken on behalf of the Special Operations Executive (SOE) to the Resistance groups, before and after D-Day, paid rich dividends. As the first Allied troops landed in Normandy, so Resistance groups all over France went into action. Supply dumps were destroyed, communications (road, rail, telephone/teleprinter) were cut or disrupted. The last-named compelled the Germans to send their messages by wireless, the transmissions of which could be – and were – intercepted by the code breakers at Bletchley Park.

In conjunction with Allied air attacks, the Resistance sabotage of road and rail links, railway rolling stock, the destruction of supply dumps (notably petrol) and roadside ambushes imposed delays on German troop movements. One example is that of the infamous 2nd SS Panzer Division (*Das Reich*), which was subjected to all of the above during its move from Toulouse to Normandy. This move was expected to take three days, but actually took seventeen days to accomplish. The division's losses of vehicles during its move to Normandy were minimal, but it suffered casualties from the almost incessant sniper fire, which seemed to come from everywhere. With this and other like episodes to consider, it was evident to the Germans that they could not rely on control of their own rear areas. To have to bring reinforcements and supplies up to the battle front under the constant threat of air attack was bad enough, but to bring them through territory alive with Resistance forces was even worse. Accordingly, just when every man was needed in the Normandy battle, eight German infantry divisions were assigned to try to keep order in the rear areas. Small wonder, then, that speaking soon after the end of the war, General Dwight D Eisenhower, Supreme Commander of the Allied forces in Europe, stated that the French Resistance (which the crews of 38 Group and other formations had helped to arm) was worth fifteen divisions to him in the task of liberating France from the German Army.

Rounding out the picture of this period (June–September) on a personal level, most of my time was spent on the airbase. When not required for operations or resting after one, we were frequently engaged in exercises (glider towing, navigational etc.), air tests and, in August, the collection of gliders from the storage unit; but it was not all work and no play. When not required to fly, I could cycle out to Fairford town, occasionally to Cirencester for dancing or, most frequently, to Swindon, where I was a member of the YCL.

Every six weeks or so we would be granted six days' leave, when I would return to Acton and my parents, meet local friends who were still there, and go dancing at the Hammersmith Palais. I even acquired two girlfriends (at different times) while back home. One such leave was enlivened by the arrival of a V-1 flying bomb, which came down uncomfortably close to home and seriously damaged the East Acton Baptist Church, fortunately without killing anyone.

A Typical Day for a Flight Engineer

I wake up in a single iron bed, under blankets and between sheets, in a Nissen hut accommodating sixteen aircrew, all of whom are NCOs (trained in various flying 'trades' (gunners, flight engineers, navigators etc). As some of them may be sleeping after a night operation, there is no Tannoy to wake us. Our incentive to get dressed and tidy up ourselves is to get to the Sergeants' Mess in time for breakfast.

After a leisurely meal we start down to our respective flight offices (more huts), in my case to join fellow flight engineers and the engineering officer in charge of us, together with any commissioned flight engineers (a rare breed). There we would sit, hear any orders for the day and chat informally, in what I now realise was a wasted opportunity for us to be required to speak about any problems encountered while in the air. Experiences thus shared might have been of value had we met with a similar problem ourselves when flying. In fact, my most vivid memory of these get-togethers occurred one cold winter when it became my turn to light the hut's pot-bellied stove, using only twisted pieces of newspaper to ignite the coke! Of course, there was never any allocation of firewood for the purpose. Again, we were never ordered or encouraged to visit the hangars where our aircraft were being serviced. Had we done so, we could well have become better at our jobs.

In later years it has always annoyed me that ninety per cent of what we learned while under training to become flight engineers, such as knowledge of electrical circuits, details of carburation, oil seals and other information essential for ground tradesmen, was useless when we were actually in the air. We needed to know how to deal with the snags which could arise when we were flying, and most of my knowledge of these was gained while actually in the air, working in cooperation with the pilot and other members of the crew. I imagine that they had similar problems, but perhaps not as great as mine.

Our afternoons were usually quite relaxed, if we were not due for an operation that night. Often, we were sent up for an air test of a Stirling, or towing a glider to give the glider pilots practice in being towed, flying, releasing and landing. Evenings were usually our own, to spend in the leisure area of the Sergeants' Mess, in a pub at Fairford (Dunmow, later), or occasionally at a dance either in the local town or on the station, when girls would be ferried in from Fairford town and the surrounding district. I would also regularly attend the meetings of Swindon YCL, where we would discuss politics.

After our move to Great Dunmow, in October, we would attend the local 'hops' in the village, or cycle to Braintree for a better dance. My companion on these trips was invariably Bob Sutton, our bomb aimer. Later, at Dunmow, a discussion group was organised by our padre, to discuss the type of Britain we wished to see after the war.

The Battle of Arnhem

The weather in the early part of September was quite good, and our supply operations over France were mostly flown without interference from that quarter. Over a period of weeks we had also flown a series of glider-towing exercises, which had steadily increased in size and complexity. We had been warned for a number of airborne operations which were then 'scrubbed', due to the swift advance of the Allied ground forces through France, Belgium and up to the Dutch border. Finally, we were briefed and held in readiness for an operation that was not cancelled: Operation 'Market Garden', the airborne and ground invasion of Holland. This has been fully covered elsewhere, so this account will be confined to our own part in the operation.

Nos. 38 and 46 Groups of the RAF were tasked with towing the glider-borne elements of the British 1st Airborne Division to the Dutch city of Arnhem, where they were to capture and hold the road bridge (the 'bridge too far') spanning the Lower Rhine, thereby opening an entrance into Germany for the Allied ground forces advancing from the south. H-hour (when the first gliders were due to land) was set for 1300 hrs Continental time (one hour ahead of GMT). The date, when finally chosen, was 17 September.

The operation was to proceed this way. Twenty minutes before H-hour, twelve Stirlings of 190 and 620 Squadrons were to drop 'pathfinder' troops of the 21st Independent Parachute Company on the selected landing and drop zones. Once on the ground, the troops were to set up Eureka beacons, onto which the Rebecca receivers in our aircraft would home, lay out the identification letters of the LZ/DZ, a landing 'T' composed of large white panels, to indicate the wind direction, and prepare smoke canisters, which would also indicate wind direction.

The pathfinder troops had three areas to mark. LZ 'S', some five miles west of the Arnhem bridge, was situated just to the north

Arnhem-bound paratroops of the 21st Independent Parachute Company wait at Fairford to board their aircraft.
Photograph courtesy of the Imperial War Museum, London

of the Arnhem–Utrecht railway line, and would be covered by six Stirlings of 620 Squadron, led by Squadron Leader Bunker. Just to the south of the railway and west of Wolfheze were LZ 'Z' and the adjacent DZ 'X'. These were to be covered by six Stirlings of 190 Squadron, led by Squadron Leader Gilliard. At H-hour the first of 153 Horsa gliders were to begin landing on LZ 'S', having been towed there by 130 Dakotas of HS (Heavy Supply) Group and twenty-three Albermarles of 38 Group. From H plus 19 minutes, Stirlings and Halifax's of 38 Group would bring in 154 Horsa and thirteen Hamilcar gliders to LZ 'Z'. Our own squadron (nineteen Stirlings) was due over the LZ at H plus 34 minutes. The paratroops were timed to arrive over DZ 'X' at H plus 50 minutes, being lifted by 143 Dakotas of the American IX Troop Carrier Command, which would be operating from bases in Lincolnshire.

There were many other details in the briefing, but looking back, now, my main memory is of the map on the wall of the briefing hut, with the pinned tape reaching out from Fairford, across England, the North Sea and deep into Holland.

The morning of 17 September was generally fine over Fairford, with only small patches of broken cloud. With our flight equipment – mine being a tool bag and my chute – we aircrews were ferried out to our aircraft, which were diagonally lined up on both sides of the runway, on which the gliders were lined up in two staggered files. We would be flying our usual Stirling (LK405 W-Willie) with the addition of a seventh crew member, a Flight Sergeant Backhouse, who would be flying with us as second pilot. On the nose of our Stirling the number '437' was chalked; this number also being chalked on the nose of the glider we were to tow. Our glider would carry seven troops, a jeep, a trailer and a heavy motorcycle.

The first aircraft to take off were the twelve Stirlings (less gliders) carrying the pathfinder troops, all of them being airborne between 1010 and 1018 hrs. After a pause of several minutes, the first Stirling/Horsa combination (Wing Commander Harrison) became airborne at 1025 hrs, followed in quick succession by the rest of us, our crew leaving the ground at 1033 hrs.

Instead of immediately setting course for Holland, as might be supposed, we first flew westwards to the Bristol Channel, where the squadron turned about and closed up to form a stream. We flew back over Fairford at 2,500 ft (the height for the outward journey) then set course for Hatfield, where our stream joined those of other squadrons. From there we flew across England to Aldeburgh, where we crossed the English coast and flew out to sea. It was a bright, sunny day and looking down at the green fields of England, giving way to the calm and sparkling sea over which our air armada was flying, put me in a happy mood. A further encouragement was the sight of the rescue launches stationed at regular intervals along our route. Anyone being forced to 'ditch' in the sea would have a very good chance of being rescued. In fact, as we progressed to Holland, we did see three gliders down on the sea. The occupants of one glider were being taken off by a rescue launch; the people of the other two gliders had apparently already been rescued. One launch, positioned in the middle of the North Sea, was equipped with a Eureka beacon. It was here that the Albermarles and their gliders, operating from the forward base at Manston, would join the main stream, some of them coming to Arnhem with us and the rest going to Nijmegen, where the American 82nd Airborne Division was landing.

About forty minutes after leaving the English coast, we crossed the Dutch coast over Schouwen Island. From there, our route took us past Breda and Tilburg to a point south of 's-Hertogenbosch, where we turned north-east for the final leg to Arnhem. A small amount of flak was seen at one point, but not close enough to be of personal concern to ourselves. However, two of our squadron's aircraft did suffer slight flak damage, but no casualties. The flak position responsible was taken care of by some of the escorting fighters flying with us. And not a single German fighter in sight!

We duly arrived at our assigned landing zone. This was LZ 'Z', a little to the west of Wolfheze and some six miles west of the Arnhem bridge. The LZ was a scene of a confused mass of gliders. On the ground, gliders laying in the fields and pointing in all directions. In the air, other gliders were coasting down to land and many more being towed in behind us. At 1336 hrs, when two

Stirling/Horse combinations crossing in over the Dutch coast.
Photograph courtesy of the Imperial War Museum, London

Gliders on Landing Zone 'S', five miles west of the Arnhem road bridge.
Photograph courtesy of the Imperial War Museum

miles south-west of the LZ, our glider waggled its wings and cast off and joined the others making their way down. For us, a last view of the scene, the tugs ahead of us releasing their tow ropes, those behind with their gliders, stretching far into the distance, the nearer ones releasing, and that confused scene below. My own view was somewhat restricted, as I was looking out of the astrodome, my usual position over enemy territory, while trying to keep an eye on my instruments.

We dropped our tow rope and then, as briefed, made a 180° climbing turn to port, making way for the incoming aircraft. Levelling off at 7,000 ft and following the same route as that flown outbound, we settled down to an uneventful flight back to Fairford, where we landed at 1553 hrs. All of our squadron's aircraft returned safely. One aircraft was forced to return early, when its glider cast off over South Cerney airfield, possibly due to its load shifting, which would have threatened the glider's safety. After debriefing and a meal, we adjourned to the mess, where we chatted with our friends and some of the remaining glider pilots, who would be going to Arnhem the following day.

As an illustration of the mishaps that could befall a glider operation, the following may be of interest. Of the 320 gliders bound for Arnhem on the first day of 'Market Garden', thirty-six were unsuccessful. Of these, seventeen suffered broken tow ropes; five cast off when their tugs developed engine trouble; twelve cast off for various other reasons, such as loads shifting; one was damaged before take-off, and one broke up in mid-air over England and crashed, killing all on board. This last was, thankfully, an extremely rare occurrence.

The pattern of 18 September followed that of the previous day, except that due to persistent mist over Fairford and many other airfields, we took off four hours later than planned. This day, our squadron was briefed to tow 21 gliders to LZ 'X', which had been used the previous day as DZ 'X'. Our first aircraft eventually took off at 1151 hrs, and we were all airborne by 1215 hrs.

We again followed the northern route over Holland. However, unlike the previous day, when we had been virtually unopposed, this time we met with a good deal of flak when we crossed the Dutch coast and at intervals on our way to the landing zone, where it became quite intense. Our luck held and we arrived over LZ 'X' without having suffered any flak damage. We were greeted by a scene of confusion similar to that of the previous day. Gliders already down were pointing in all directions, but this time mingled with the parachutes of the previous day's para' drop. Other gliders were casting off and descending towards the landing area, and more still coming in behind us. There was an additional feature: unlike the day before, when the landings had been virtually unopposed, this day the gliders were making their approach and landing under enemy fire. Our glider cast off safely and started down, whereupon we dropped our tow rope and turned thankfully for home, which we reached without further incident. All of our squadron's aircraft returned safely, one of them with flak damage. Four of our gliders were unsuccessful, three with broken tow ropes (two of these over Holland), and the fourth casting off when the tug developed engine trouble soon after taking off.

In addition to its operation to LZ 'X' (203 gliders delivered), 38 Group also despatched a force of Stirlings to drop supplies on LZ 'L', an open space in woodland north-east of Oosterbeek. Dakotas of 46 Group delivered sixty-nine gliders to LZ 'S', where the gliders were forced to land among those that had arrived the day before. Finally, 115 Dakotas of the USAAF dropped paratroops on DZ 'Y', located on Ginkel Heath and almost nine miles west of the Arnhem bridge.

These operations were carried out for the loss (all to flak) of twelve aircraft: three Stirlings, one RAF Dakota and eight USAAF Dakotas. A fourth Stirling was written off when it crashed on take-off. Enemy fighters had been up in some numbers, but they were held off by strong Allied fighter screens, and we saw nothing of them.

The following day (19 September), our crew was stood down from operations, the only flying for us being an air test. The squadron effort for this day was in two parts. Sixteen Stirlings were detailed to drop supplies on DZ 'V', in the north-western outskirts of Arnhem itself, while two other Stirlings were to tow gliders to LZ 'X', the gliders being aborts from the previous day. Bad weather again enforced a delay, and it was early afternoon before the aircraft took off.

The first indication that things were going wrong came when the aircraft, with two missing and several others damaged by flak, returned to Fairford. In due course, we who had not flown to Arnhem that day met the returned crews in the mess. Then we learned of the reception they had met – flak all over the shop – and of the crews who had not returned. The route taken this day and on subsequent resupply flights was the southern one, which was Manston-Ostend-Ghent, then turning over Belgium to fly up the Airborne corridor via Eindhoven and Nijmegen and thence to Arnhem. Our first loss was suffered over the corridor, when Flight Sergeant Coeshott's aircraft was shot down by flak and crashed at Sint-Michielsgestel, south-east of 's-Hertogenbosch. There were no survivors. The second loss was Squadron Leader Gilliard, whose Stirling took two heavy flak hits when over the drop zone. The crew baled out, and three of them eventually returned to England. A fourth crew member was taken prisoner, but the pilot and two others were killed.

Had we but known so at the time, the ground situation at Arnhem was worse than we thought. A message from the 1st Airborne, saying that the selected drop zone was no longer in their hands and nominating another area, had not been received in England. The aircrews, also, had been instructed to ignore ground signals elsewhere, as they might be German decoys. In consequence, all of the supplies dropped fell into German hands, although some were later recovered. It was over this drop zone, this day, that Flight Lieutenant David Lord of 271 Squadron (Dakotas) won a posthumous Victoria Cross.

The official account of the British airborne divisions, *By Air to Battle*, says of the aircraft coming in to drop their supplies on that Tuesday: 'They were met by a screen of flak and it was awe-inspiring to see them fly straight into it – straight into a flaming hell!' (Lieutenant-Colonel M Saint Parke, who had watched the episode from Oosterbeek).

It needs little repeating that those who had returned, and we who listened to them, were definitely not happy about the prospect of going to Arnhem again on the morrow. Many of the others stayed in the mess, drinking to cheer themselves up. I, however, have never been much of a drinker and I soon left, to go to my billet and read until lights out.

Back from Arnhem, 17 September.
Wing Commander G E Harrison (commanding 190 Squadron) reports to Group Captain A H Wheeler, the station commander of RAF Fairford.
Photograph courtesy of the Imperial War Museum

The following day we were one of seventeen squadron crews briefed for another resupply operation to Arnhem. The drop zone for this operation was a road junction 200 yards to the west of the Hartenstein Hotel (now the Airborne Museum) at nearby Oosterbeek. The drop was to be carried out by sixty-four Dakotas of 46 Group (which would make their drops first) and sixty-seven Stirlings of 38 Group. We were warned to expect intense flak over the drop zone. Possibly to avoid congestion at the Hartenstein site, thirty-three other Stirlings were to make their drops on LZ 'Z', which had not been used since the first day of the Arnhem operation. We duly joined our aircraft, then had a long wait before being given the order to move off. Our crew eventually took off at 1512 hrs.

Being an ordinary person, who had no real reason to be afraid, I was not usually subject to fear, but I must admit that I was most definitely fearful as we flew up that Allied corridor in Holland, not knowing what would happen when we left the comparative safety of Allied-held territory. Leave it we did, of course, and we were soon passing over a German flak position. My fear gone, I gazed down at it, and as we were flying at low-level – about 500 ft – I could plainly see the German gun crews running about, manning the guns and firing up at us. In addition to the long-range heavy guns, such as the 88 mm type, the German Flak Arm also operated large numbers of 20 mm and 37 mm quick-firing guns (light and medium flak). It was possibly a 37 mm shell bursting in front of us that sent a piece of shrapnel flying through the bomb aimer's compartment, just missing his head and smashing some of the electrical equipment fixed to the side of the aircraft there. I walked forward to look down into the compartment and saw Bob, our bomb aimer, grinning up at me and pointing to the damage caused.

We duly sighted the drop zone, and the aircraft ahead of us began flying into the flak. At this point I left my normal crew position and made my way to the rear of the aircraft. One of the duties of a flight engineer was to act as a dispatcher, and on this occasion we were carrying two panniers in addition to our usual load of twenty-four containers. By the weight of them the panniers must have held ammunition, as I could hardly move them with my hands. The large oblong 'jump' exit in the floor of

Supply container arriving on a drop zone at Arnhem.
Photograph courtesy of the Imperial War Museum

the aircraft had been opened, so I decided to lie down on the floor and push the panniers out with my feet when I was given the order to do so by the green light signal above me.

Therefore, I did not see the scene as we crossed the Rhine and made for the drop zone. I was aware, however, of the flak, for the air was full of the noise of exploding shells, and I could hear the sound of shrapnel hitting our aircraft more or less continually; but our luck held and we were not hit in any vital part. Soon, the green light came on, and by pushing with my legs and straightening my knees I was able to push out the first pannier. I then moved over and, in a similar fashion, disposed of the second pannier. Looking back now, and knowing the problem at the DZ, I am pretty sure that I had made a present of at least one of those panniers to the Germans…

With the panniers gone, I wound in the static lines of their parachutes, checked that the jumping exit was closed, then quickly made my way back to my own crew position. Ikey had opened the throttles to take-off boost and we were climbing steeply. Below, I caught a glimpse of the battlefield, mostly covered in smoke. But my attention and that of the crew was directed mainly towards the Stirling which was following us up, for its port outer engine was smoking and, far worse, the port wing was on fire. We watched as it slowly levelled out, turned and began to go down. Then the parachutes started to come out, and I counted them as the aircraft descended: one, two, three, four, five… but no more did I see. To my mind, the pilot had held on while his crew got out, but had no time to jump himself. As for us, we were now nearly in the clear, with just a short distance of enemy territory to cover. Regaining the Allied corridor we received little further attention from the German flak, and we landed at Fairford at 2000 hrs.

The scene in the mess that evening was similar to that of the evening before; stories from those of us who had returned, mixed with fact and rumour about those who had not made it back. Three squadron crews were missing, but this was soon reduced to two. One of the missing Stirlings, flown by Flight Lieutenant Robertson, had been hard hit by flak when over the drop zone. The aircraft was barely controllable, but with the aid of the bomb aimer the pilot nursed it to the airfield at Ghent (in British hands), where he made a successful belly landing without serious injury to the crew, who were soon back at Fairford.

The Stirling we saw go down was being flown by Flying Officer Le Bouvier, and all of the crew survived. The bomb aimer, wireless operator, flight engineer and two Army dispatchers were captured, but the others successfully evaded capture and regained the British lines. A correspondent of the *Daily Telegraph* newspaper had been flying with them this day, and he also made it back. The third loss (Flying Officer Matheson) was shot down by flak and crashed at Doorwerth. There were no survivors.

Our crew was most fortunate to be stood down the following day (21 September), for the stories of the few crews returning from this day's operation were really bad.

The day began with ten squadron crews being briefed for a second supply drop at Oosterbeek. This time, the drop zone was to be at the Hartenstein itself, an indication of how the Airborne perimeter at Oosterbeek had shrunk since the previous day. The operation was to be carried out by fifty-three Dakotas, followed by sixty-four Stirlings, these flying in three boxes of two squadrons each. Our squadron would be flying at the rear of the third box. An escort of six squadrons of Spitfires was to be provided, two squadrons of which would cover each box of Stirlings.

Over Holland the operation began to go badly wrong for our squadron with the non-arrival of their fighter escort which, unknown to our crews, was weathered in at their bases. The German flak was as active as ever, especially at Oosterbeek. Finally, for the first and only time during the Arnhem operation, German fighters were present in some numbers, and with the flak they had a field day of it, shooting down our aircraft like clay pigeons. Of the ten squadron aircraft that had set out for Oosterbeek, only three (all of them damaged) made it back to Fairford. Of the missing aircrews, the following was later learned.

Wing Commander Harrison's aircraft was shot down by flak and crashed at Zettin. The flight engineer (Sergeant Percy) was the only survivor, but with serious injuries. With the help of other shot down aircrew and a Dutch lady doctor, he finally reached the British lines, but died of his injuries very soon afterwards.

Pilot Officer Herger also crashed at Zettin after being shot down by flak. The flight engineer and air gunner survived to be taken prisoner, both of them wounded. The other crew members were all killed.

Flight Lieutenant Anderson was shot down by flak and fighters. He ditched in the River Maas, near Demen, but the Stirling broke up and quickly sank, leaving only three survivors.

Flying Officer Beberfield's aircraft was also shot down by flak and fighters. It crashed at Herveld without survivors.

Pilot Officer Farren's aircraft was hit over the drop zone by flak and then attacked by fighters. He remained with the aircraft and crashed at Wijchen, receiving serious back injuries. Three of the crew baled out, but two were injured on landing. The three other crew members were killed after baling out too low.

Flying Officer Pascoe was hit by flak when over the drop zone. He forced landing at Grave without any injuries to the crew, all of whom duly returned to Fairford.

Flying Officer Hay crashed at Tilburg, cause unknown. All of the crew survived to be taken prisoner.

Losses for the Stirling force as a whole totalled fourteen, their highest losses of the Arnhem operation. This was brought about largely by the English weather. In the early morning, England had been covered by widespread, thick fog and low stratus, which had cleared over the south midlands by 1000 hrs, allowing the Dakotas and Stirlings to take off as planned. But in the east, where the escorting fighters were based, the bad weather persisted until the afternoon, when the stratus lifted and visibility improved.

Of the escorts, Nos. 64 and 126 Squadrons, operating from Bradwell Bay, were detailed to cover the first box of Stirlings. They took off with difficulty and were delayed in reaching the rendezvous, finally catching up with their charges on the run-up to the drop zone. From there, their Stirlings were escorted back to Ostend without incident.

Nos. 504 and 611 Squadrons, operating from Manston and Bradwell Bay respectively, were detailed for the second box. Six of 611's Spitfires took off but were unable to form up, and four aborted. The remaining two went on as far as Dordrecht without sighting the Stirlings before turning back. 504 Squadron was weathered in and did not take off.

Nos. 350 and 402 Squadrons, operating from Hawkinge and detailed for the third box, were weathered in and did not take off.

The consequences for the Stirling squadrons are noted below.

		Desp	Abort	FTR	Dam	Cause
First box	299 Sqdn	11	1	1	2	Flak
	570 Sqdn	11	1	-	3	Flak
Second box	295 Sqdn	11	-	1	?	Flak
	620 Sqdn	11	-	2	2	Flak/fighters
Third box	196 Sqdn	10	1	3	1	Flak/fighters
	190 Sqdn	10	-	7	3	Flak/fighters
Totals:		64	3	14	11 plus (?)	N/A

The Dakotas of 46 Group also had a rough time. In addition to attacking the rear Stirling formations, the German fighters also engaged the first wave of Dakotas returning from Oosterbeek. Between them, the fighters and flak accounted for thirteen Dakotas, and compelled others to make forced landings in Belgium. A further loss was suffered when the port wing of a Dakota was torn off under the impact of a supply canister dropped from an aircraft flying above.

The atmosphere in the mess was very gloomy that evening, many of us being upset by the loss of good friends and apprehensive of what the following day might bring to the remainder of our squadron and to our colleagues on 620 Squadron.

I had an appointment in Swindon that evening and decided to go, in spite of everything. The Government had recently relaxed the blackout (the forbidding of outside lights at night, in force since the beginning of the war) to a 'dim out', which allowed a certain amount of light. I saw this for the first time when I entered Swindon that evening. I attended my meeting and discussed politics with my comrades there, not mentioning a single word about Arnhem.

Our fears of what the morrow might bring were groundless. No operation was called for and the whole squadron was stood down. In fact, I never had to fly to Arnhem again. Instead, this day we flew to Northolt, near London, to transport an officer to the BBC studios, where he was interviewed and told the British people something of the Arnhem operation and of his own experiences when flying there. And, as my diary notes, we were subsequently relieved by the return of a number of our comrades who had been shot down, but had survived and returned safely. I heard many stories, of course, of their adventures, but I can now remember only one. This concerned a squadron leader who had been shot down on the south bank of the Rhine. In making his way back to Allied lines, he had collected many stragglers and reached safety, bringing with him a sizeable body of men. He was later awarded the Military Medal, a decoration normally awarded only to the Army.

We later heard that on 21 September the German fighters had not had things entirely their own way. Two squadron gunners each claimed the destruction of a fighter – one Me 109 and one FW 190. The Germans later admitted the loss of three Me 109s.

Early in the morning of 23 September, the 1st Airborne sent an urgent request for a supply drop at the Hartenstein. A force of fifty-six Dakotas and seventy-three Stirlings was sent out, to which our squadron contributed seven Stirlings – all that could be put up with the memory of the previous operation fresh in our minds. We awaited their return with apprehension.

The fighter cover this day was strong and continuous, and the German fighters were unable to get through to the supply-dropping aircraft, which flew almost to Oosterbeek before meeting serious opposition. Instead of engaging individual aircraft, as hitherto, the German flak now put up a barrage over the approach lane through which our aircraft were forced to fly.

Three Stirlings and two Dakotas were shot down in the Oosterbeek area, and three more Stirlings came down later in the ground corridor, but all of our squadron's Stirlings returned safely, some of them with slight flak damage.

And so ended our part in the Arnhem operation, an operation that had cost our squadron dearly. Twelve Stirlings had been lost or written off with battle damage, and the human cost was thirty-eight killed and thirteen taken prisoner. A further twenty men (some of them injured) evaded capture and regained Allied lines but, sadly, one of these men died of his injuries as he reached safety, and is numbered with the dead. Also among the dead were our commanding officer, Wing Commander Harrison, and the senior flight commander, Squadron Leader Gilliard. The squadron was now under the temporary command of the remaining flight commander, Squadron Leader Gibb, pending the arrival of a new commanding officer.

Apart from the passage quoted earlier from the official account of the airborne forces, I have refrained from quoting others in this account of the Arnhem operation, but I cannot resist including here the experience of a friend and fellow veteran of the battle, Para Des Evans of the 1st Airborne Recce Squadron, who wrote:

> The flight over the North Sea provided a spectacle that no one who was there will ever forget. As far as the eye could see, there were planes and gliders all travelling on a dead straight course. Weaving in and out, up and down, were the fighters; there seemed to be hundreds of them ... Somehow, Sunday seemed to be a strange day for such a trip, but most of us felt a great elation now that we were committed to an operation. This one would not be aborted now. We were all raring to go, superbly fit and full of the feeling that we were invincible...

My diary entries for the week read as follows:

> Sunday, 17 September
>
> Towed glider to invasion of Holland. What a sight. Saw most of the incidents that the papers recorded.

Monday, 18 September

Towed another glider. More opposition this time. Too much flak for my liking.

Tuesday, 19 September

Stood down. Heard many nasty tales about flak around DZ. Lost S/L Gilliard.

Wednesday, 20 September

Went to Arnhem with containers – saw other kites go down. Collected flak. Did not like it. Lost Alderson and Kershaw.

Thursday, 21 September

Off again. Lost seven crews out of ten. Went to Swindon in eve and saw 'dim out'. Was miserable.

Friday, 22 September

Off again. Feel better. Mess dance in eve. Had a beer or two and a dance or two. Not bad.

Saturday, 23 September

Alderson came back from dead – crash-landed apparently. Good news of others too.

Memo: a week of history, but too personal to be comfortable.

Further Afield

With the end of the Arnhem operation, our squadron resumed the task of supplying the Resistance groups in enemy-occupied Europe, Two supply operations were flown in late September. For the first, we were one of seven crews detailed for a supply drop in France. The operation was unsuccessful, there being no reception, and we were all forced to bring back our loads. A few nights later, nine crews operated over Holland, five being successful and the others having no reception.

These operations apart, the remainder of September and October were taken up with the training of new crews, which included a daylight paratroop drop, day and night container dropping, air to sea firing on a fixed range and fighter affiliation. Acceptance checks on new aircraft were carried out, as were air tests of aircraft that had been damaged at Arnhem. At the same time, a number of aircrew who had been shot down during the operation returned to the squadron. The beginning of October brought a new commanding officer, when Wing Commander R H Bunker was posted in from 620 Squadron, where he had been a flight commander.

In the first week of October, we were briefed for a glider tow to Italy (Operation 'Molten'), which required sixteen aircraft each from 190 and 620 Squadrons. The first leg of the journey would take us to Istres, near Marseille, where we would refuel and stop overnight. From there, the following day, we were to fly to Ciampino (Rome), release the gliders there then continue to Pomigliano (Naples), where we would land. The whole operation, including the return flight, was expected to take three days. It actually took four days. Bad weather imposed a delay of two days, and the operation finally got under way on 9 October.

The route took us into the Cherbourg peninsular and then deep into France – mile after mile and hour after hour, in warm sunshine, lulled by the even sound of our engines. Suddenly, Ikey

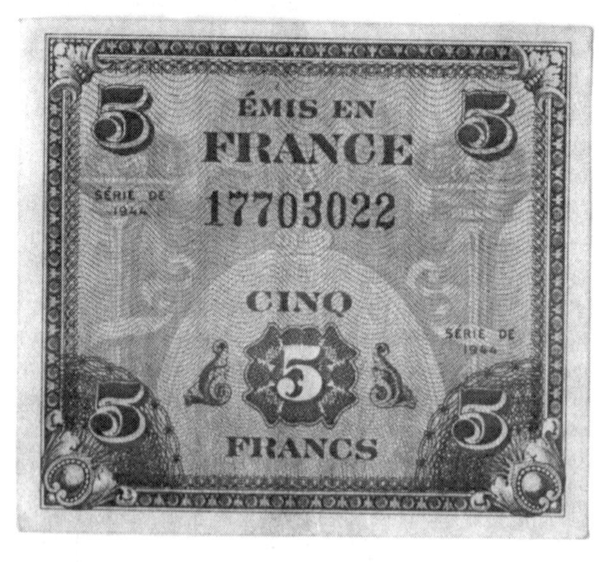

Military money, issued to aircrews and accepted in liberated countries.

called over the intercom, 'Malc, the controls have stuck – I can't move them!' Remember, we were towing a glider.

I jumped up and began to trace the rudder and elevator cables back towards the rear of the aircraft. Indeed, they would not move, but I could find nothing wrong, no jamming, no obstruction – nothing! Getting to the back, I plugged my intercom into the socket there and reported that I could find nothing wrong.

'It's OK,' said Ikey, 'I fell asleep and my elbow knocked the automatic pilot on!' Collapse of stout – but dim – flight engineer!

We finally reached our airfield, near the village of Istres, by the Mediterranean. After a meal, we made our way down to the village, where we had some wine in a café. There, I met and endeavoured to chat to some of the locals.

The next day, we took off and flew out over the Mediterranean, past Corsica to the coast of Italy. Slightly inland, we turned and followed the coast down to Rome. After our glider had safely cast off, we circled over the city, especially the Vatican, as most unusual sightseers, before flying down to Naples, catching a glimpse of Vesuvius before landing. Accommodation had been arranged beforehand, and we were put up on board one of the troopships lying in the harbour.

We proceeded to explore the city, and found the people to be most friendly. One young girl insisted on blowing the whistle attached to the top button of my battledress blouse (to be blown if lost in a dinghy at sea, or in the sea itself), which entailed her head being in close proximity to mine! We spent some time in a classical palace, which had been acquired as a NAAFI for the use of servicemen. Afterwards, we spent the evening at the Teatro San Carlo to see *Tosca*.

Some of the lads, either drunk on the wine or trigger-happy (having never used a pistol in anger), and being in a country formerly our enemy, were a little aggressive. One evening, as we walked back to the ship, we passed a shuttered shop, and in the gloom behind sat two men. The lads saw something suspicious in this and ordered them out. This the men refused to do – or did not understand the order – so one of the lads attempted to shoot the lock off the shutters. The bullet ricocheted up the road, missing

Naples. Vesuvius can be seen in the distance.

people walking along the top. At this, we managed to get our people to leave and join the ship.

This welcome break soon ended and we returned to Britain, carrying repatriated servicemen and flying over the Alps on the way, returning to Fairford on the afternoon of 12 October.

Norway

With France, Belgium but only part of Holland liberated, attention now turned to that latter country and Norway. A few days after our return from Italy the squadron moved to Great Dunmow, in Essex, which had previously been occupied by an American bomber group. Our new base was a little nearer to Norway which, however, was still on the other side of the North Sea and about four hours' flying time away. Navigation became more difficult, especially when Norway was cloud-covered. Also, the sea provided no location points. But we had a very good navigator in Ross, and we never became lost. I do, however, remember some swift map work on one trip when we hit the Norwegian coast unexpectedly. My own problem was that of fuel, as the Stirling's full fuel load gave about 8½ hours' flight endurance, and a trip to Norway and back would take about eight hours, mostly over the sea.

Settling in at our new base then waiting for the next moon period, it was the end of October before the squadron operated again, when nine aircraft were sent to various drop zones in Holland. At about this time Ikey, who had risen in rank to warrant officer, was commissioned as a pilot officer.

I would like to try to describe the experience of being in a large bomber – the Short Stirling – at night, on a long flight. Imagine a quite warm metal interior, as wide as a coach, lit only by the lights over the instruments and perhaps the moon and the stars, vibrating and gently undulating as it flies and the noise of the four 1,600 hp engines muffled by our flying helmets. Only rarely does anyone speak, and when they do it is usually some instruction relevant to flying. From where I sit (on an iron bar, as the engineer's seat has been removed for ease of abandoning the aircraft if need be) I can see Ron, the wireless operator, across the way and, looking forward, glimpse the side of Ross, the navigator, sitting at his map table. Up front are the backs of the high seats of the pilot (Ikey) and Bob, the bomb aimer, who acts as second pilot. Above me is the astrodome, through which I can see the sky. On one occasion, Ross pointed out to me the red giant star Betelgeuse, in the constellation of Orion, which he preferred to use to obtain a star 'fix', to ascertain where the aircraft was in the sky. To the rear is the dark body of the aircraft, but I cannot see beyond the internal wing struts, which cross the fuselage a few feet away. Way down the back is the chemical Elsan toilet and beyond that is our lonely rear gunner, Arthur, sitting isolated in his turret. In front of me is my bank of instruments, which I have to monitor. Every twenty minutes I have to fill in a log entry from the panel. If I change fuel tanks, or if the engine conditions change, I must log that as well. The aircraft is not waterproof, and if it is raining raindrops fall across my log sheet. I look out of the astrodome occasionally to ensure that all is well with the wings and the engines, being able to get a good view of them from that position. I can also see the blackness below, which is the sea.

Hours later, if we are fortunate, we catch a glimpse of the coast of Denmark (in German hands) off the starboard bow, which gives the navigator and the bomb aimer a reference point, but we are just as likely to miss it and carry on until we hit the coast of Norway. Here again, the navigator can correct our course by reference to his map. We change course to fly up the Skagerrak. On one trip, we passed over a German flak ship, which blazed up at us ineffectually. We met it again on the way back, when it detected us earlier than before and gave us a good display of fireworks, which made us take violent evasive action.

Usually, our target would lay among the mountains to the north of Oslo, and where the Norwegian resistance hid and operated. We flew to Norway many times but, as it would be boring to deal separately with each flight, I will condense these trips into one. Crossing the coast near Oslo (a reference point) we turned towards our target. This heading took us near to the German airfield at Gardermoen. We were disconcerted to see below the profile of a Junkers Ju 88 night fighter crossing our path. However, the German crew must have been concentrating on their landing approach, for they did not see us. And so we flew on to our drop zone in a mountain valley, where after the usual exchange of recognition signals, we made a successful drop of our eighteen containers. Then, it was up and away, back to the Skagerrak and home, obtaining a 'fix' from the last corner of the Norwegian coast as we cleared the Skagerrak and began our crossing of the dark, wide North Sea.

Returning from a similar operation and flying at 10,000 ft, we entered cloud and the temperature dropped rapidly. Being fearful of ice, I pushed my head and an Aldis lamp into the astrodome and looked out towards the wings. With the aid of the lamp, I could see that ice was indeed beginning to form on the wings, and if allowed to build up would destroy all lift and crash the aircraft. I therefore asked Ikey to descend to a warmer altitude. However, the ice continued to increase, and we had to keep descending through the cloud until, according to the altimeter, we were only 200 ft above the sea. Working on air pressure, the altimeter could not give an accurate reading unless it was reset to the local barometric pressure which, in this case, was unavailable, as no weather ships were stationed in the North Sea. We may have been at 200 ft, above or below, we did not know. Being this dangerously near to the sea, we dared not descend further into the blackness, so we flew on until the ice finally broke off and fell away, leaving us free to climb. But these manoeuvres had left us short of fuel, and I reported this to Ikey. He and Ross then altered course for the east coast of Scotland, where we made a good landfall, finally landing at the RAF base of Kinloss. As earlier remarked, we went to Norway many times but the other operations while long, hard and tiring, but mainly successful, passed off without undue incident.

Early in November, our crew took part in a sea search. This was for a Stirling from Rivenhall, piloted by the station commander, Group Captain W E Surplice, which had failed to return from a supply drop over Norway. No trace of the missing aircraft or its crew was found, and the search was eventually abandoned. Much later, it was learned that the Stirling had crashed in Norway as the result of icing. The aircraft went out of control and the order to abandon was given. This the crew safely did, with the exception of the pilot, who crashed with the aircraft and was killed. Of the six survivors, five evaded capture and reached Sweden with the help of the Norwegian resistance; but the sixth (the flight engineer) was captured.

When flying, one did not have to be on operations to be in danger. One clear late autumn day, we took 'W-Willie' (our usual aircraft) up for an air test. We climbed steadily and levelled out at 10,000 ft. Monitoring my instruments, I was amazed to see the engines begin to fail as their oil pressure, normally 80 lb per square inch, dropped to between 50 and 40 lb and the cylinder temperatures rose alarmingly. When the oil pressure of one engine went down to 35 lb (the engine now in danger of seizing up) I called to Ikey for it to be feathered. This involved shutting down the engine, then turning the propeller blades into the line of flight, thus preventing the propeller from 'windmilling', which would produce vibration and drag. Soon after, a second engine became dangerous and had to be feathered, and then a third. We really went to panic stations when the last engine also began to overheat, for that could obviously not be feathered, as the aircraft was already almost unflyable. It was necessary to get down as soon as possible and slow the plane down, so I asked for the flaps and undercarriage to be lowered and for the remaining engine to be throttled back and its propeller to be set at fine pitch, thereby easing the strain on it. When that had been done we practically fell out of the sky. Reaching a lower altitude, I ventured to restart an engine. Its condition stabilising, I tried restarting another engine and successfully so. By this time we were near enough to the ground and the airfield to attempt a landing, which we did on three engines (a fairly straightforward procedure), safely and thankfully.

The next day, the ground crew told me the reason for our problem. They had omitted to fix the winter baffle plates to the radiator oil coolers, to cut down the intake of air. In the cold high air, the oil in these coolers had frozen, putting them out of action. A bypass valve had then returned the hot oil straight back to the engines, overheating them and reducing the oil pressure. I had had no idea of what was wrong, but luckily my instinctive actions had saved the engines and allowed the oil to unfreeze.

Another non-operational incident involving a squadron aircrew had a tragic outcome. Four crews had been detailed for night circuits and landings with gliders. The weather, which at first had been fair, deteriorated as the detail proceeded, and only four lifts were completed. The Stirling flown by Flying Officer Kidgell first hit a tree then flew into high-tension cables before crashing in the airfield circuit, killing all on board. Four of the crew had slept in my billet, and the following day we had the sad task of packing up the belongings they had left behind.

On the operational side, an operation could go awry before the aircraft even left the ground. One November evening, six Stirlings, bound for drop zones in Holland, were moving along the taxiway towards the runway when the leading aircraft suffered the burst of a main tyre and blocked the taxiway. The five other aircraft were close behind, and it was only with great difficulty and much loss of time that they were turned around to use another runway. All five of the aircraft eventually despatched were forty-five minutes late in taking off, and although some time was made up en route they were all thirty minutes late over their drop zones. Two aircraft were successful, but the others had no reception and brought back their loads. Weather conditions were reported as 'ideal', and no opposition of any kind was met with.

Late November brought a number of awards to squadron members for their actions on the Arnhem operation; one DSO (Wing Commander Bunker), four DFCs (Flight Lieutenant Robertson, Flying Officers Siegert, Pascoe and Sutherland) and two DFMs (Flight Sergeants Thompson and Walton). But the greatest honour to be bestowed on our squadron was the privilege to adopt, as the centrepiece of our squadron badge, the double-headed eagle displayed (full frontal, wings spread), as featured in the Civic Coat of Arms of Arnhem, this device originating in the thirteenth century. The squadron badge was authorised by His Majesty King George VI in February 1945.

Christmas and New Year

Christmas of 1944 found the British and Canadian ground forces on the western front more or less at a standstill, and the American forces striving to contain the German Ardennes offensive, better known now as the 'Battle of the Bulge'. At 0500 hours on Christmas Day, we were one of twelve squadron crews roused from our beds to be briefed for a daylight ferrying operation to Belgium, which involved transporting troops to the battle area. However, during the night thick fog had settled over our base at Great Dunmow and this persisted all day, causing the operation to be postponed for twenty-four hours. The following day was a repeat of the first, with the fog thicker than ever, which prompted a further twenty-four-hour delay. In the raid morning of the third day (27 December), it seemed that we might at last get off when the fog started to clear, but it then closed in again and the operation was eventually cancelled. The fog finally cleared the following day, and we resumed dropping supplies to the resistance groups in Holland and Norway.

January 1945 was a month of bad weather, which severely restricted operations, our squadron operating only twice that month. For the first operation, five crews (ours being one) were detailed for supply drops in Holland. On this operation, I was at my post at the astrodome, looking out as we crossed the coast, when I saw a vivid light from a northerly direction. I realised that it was a V-2, a German rocket, lifting up on its way to England – probably London. We could do nothing about it, and watched it disappear into the darkness on its deadly mission.

All of the drop zones were covered by fog or low cloud, making it impossible to see any ground signals, and the other four crews were forced to bring back their loads. Our crew, however, had better luck. A Eureka radar beacon had been set up on our drop zone and its signals were received by the Rebecca receiver in our aircraft, enabling us to home in to the drop zone. Also, a small break was seen in the cloud above the drop zone, and we successfully dropped our load through this.

The second, and last, operation that month was an unusual one for our squadron: a bombing raid, which did not include our crew. This was the first of several such operations, mounted in support of our ground forces and aimed at German troop concentrations. Although our Stirling Mark IVs were equipped for glider towing and other special duties, they retained the fuselage bomb bay and wing bomb cells of the earlier versions of this aircraft, and there was no reason why they could not carry bombs instead of supply containers.

A fortnight or so after these operations, we strolled out onto the tarmac and saw 500 lb bombs reposing on trollies and waiting to be loaded onto our aircraft. Our crew was 'on' that night for its first and, as it turned out, only bombing operation. The target was a road junction at Kalkar (due east of the Reichswald Forest), through which German troops were believed to be moving. Ten crews were detailed, each aircraft carrying twenty-one 500 lb bombs (the Stirling could carry twenty-four of these bombs).

Flying our usual aircraft, W-Willie, we took off at 2136 hours and headed for the battle front. Arriving at the target, a slight amount of flak was seen, but it was mostly too far away to be of any concern. We released our bombs and these were seen to burst in the target area. Compared with our usual operations, when we dropped supply containers by parachute from 300 to 400 feet, it was most unusual and easy to bomb from several thousand feet and then simply turn for home. Although German night fighters were still active, at this stage of the war they were not the force they had been less than a year previously, and we had no trouble from that quarter. We landed back at base at 0243 hours.

It should be realised that only a limited amount of our time was spent on operations. Other flying activities covered air tests, cross-countries (with or without a glider in tow) and other odd trips. On the ground, after attending the morning get-togethers at our respective flight offices, the rest of the day was our own, unless we were required for a flight detail or were on operations that night. Otherwise, we were free to eat, rest, read, play cards or chat, sitting round the coke stove with some of our hut mates, at which point I would like to write about some of my fellow airmen.

I have already mentioned my own crew, especially the bomb aimer, Bob, who became my main companion to dances, pubs and so forth. As a flight engineer, I came to know a number of other engineers. The senior man, 'Fingers' Alderson, had been a ground engineer in the pre-war RAF. He had much useful experience to impart and I got on well with him. His aircraft had been badly damaged over Arnhem, but the pilot managed to reach the airfield at Ghent (in British hands), where the aircraft was belly landed and subsequently written off. All of the crew returned to the squadron a few days later.

Tragically, 'Fingers' Alderson was killed immediately after the European war ended when his aircraft crashed, without survivors, near Oslo.

Another engineer that I met at this time had a most amazing story to tell. Before the war, he had made his way to Spain and joined the civil war in that country by volunteering for the International Brigade. When that war was lost, he crossed into France and joined the Foreign Legion and was posted to the French mandated territory of Syria, There, after the fall of France and the rise of the pro-German Vichy Government, he attempted to desert and make his way to friendly territory, but the French caught him and sentenced him to death. He was languishing in prison when British forces marched into Syria and he was freed. That was his story, and from the detail which came with it I was convinced of its truth. What I do know is that shortly after our conversation he was lost on operations.

Then there was 'Mac', a burly man who slept in my hut, an ex-policeman. There had been a clear-out of police who were young enough for the fighting forces, and 'Mac' had volunteered for the Air Force. He had soon gained a commission (quite difficult for flight engineers) and left our hut for the officers' accommodation. I met 'Mac' again after the war, in West London, when he had returned to the police. He had the job of holding up the traffic while I, with the Communist Party, marched through Acton!

Sometimes we would leave camp, going to the neighbouring village of Little Easton or the nearby town for entertainment. Local dances were our favourite pastime, where we could meet girls. Occasionally, girls would be ferried in for a dance in the mess. There were also WAAFs at these camp dances.

Also on the station, a discussion group had been set up, headed by the padre, to help prepare airmen for the coming peace, and I had naturally joined this group. One member of the group was a ground crew sergeant, who had been an 'MP' in the Cairo Parliament. This was an organisation which had been set up to give servicemen serving in Egypt some experience in parliamentary democracy. Unfortunately for the big brass, the Parliament had elected a Communist government! Of course, this experiment in democracy had swiftly ended, with the government 'MPs' being posted to all points of the compass. Our sergeant had ended up at Dunmow.

One evening with the group, we were deep in discussion when we heard the sound of machine gun fire. We rushed out to look round and up, but saw nothing. However, the next morning, on an air test, we saw the burnt-out remains of a Stirling scattered across a field. This had been an aircraft of 620 Squadron, which had moved with us to Great Dunmow the previous October. It was returning from a container dropping exercise at Great Sampford, Essex, and was about to join the airfield circuit, landing lights burning, when it was attacked and shot down in flames by a Junkers Ju 88 intruder which had sneaked in from the North Sea. The flight engineer managed to bale out and was the only survivor. This was one of the last – if not *the* last – aircraft to be shot down over England by intruders; a Halifax was shot down near Wittering at about the same time.

As the weather improved, so the tempo of operations quickened during February and early March. It was at about this time, early in the New Year, that I saw a V-1 flying bomb – a buzz bomb (so-called due to the noise made by its pulse-jet engine) – flying over the airfield in the direction of London. With their launching sites in France now lost to them, the V-1s were launched from over the North Sea by specially adapted Heinkel 111 bombers. Also, a number of a long-range version of the V-1 were fired from sites in Holland.

The Last Operation

The beginning of March saw our squadron operating over Holland and Norway, after which we did not operate for three weeks. In addition to our usual training details (glider circuits and landings, cross countries with or without gliders etc.), we also took part in a number of Group exercises with the other squadrons of No. 38 Group, which gradually increased in size and flight duration. These exercises were mainly intended to give the glider pilots experience of long and fatiguing tows. As a result of its heavy losses at Arnhem and the decision to increase its establishment, the Glider Pilot Regiment now had many RAF pilots (surplus to RAF requirements) in its ranks. Having been trained on powered aircraft, these pilots were relatively inexperienced on gliders. On 21 March, this period of training gave way to a spate of air tests, which involved every Stirling on the station, including the reserves.

The following morning, we were one of thirty squadron crews being briefed for a large-scale airborne operation, scheduled for 24 March – Operation 'Varsity'. This operation was to support Allied ground forces which, at 0200 hours on the 24th, would begin to cross the River Rhine west of Wesel and from there drive into the German hinterland. Two airborne divisions, the British 6th and the American 17th, together with glider-borne troops, would be put down behind the rear of the German defensive line along the river. The airborne troops were to capture, clear and hold the Diersfordter Forest (on high ground overlooking Wesel and the Rhine), secure bridges over the River Issel and then link up with the ground forces advancing from the Rhine.

Our squadron's effort was to be in two parts. Twenty-four crews (including ours) were to tow gliders to LZ 'R', immediately to the south-west of Hamminkeln. The remaining six crews, operating with 620 Squadron, would tow their gliders to LZ 'P', located between LZ 'H' and the Diersfordter Forest. Unlike the

Arnhem operation, when the airborne forces were dropped over a period of three days, on 'Varsity' they would be brought in by a single huge lift.

That afternoon, after the briefing, further air tests took place, and by the end of the day the squadron had thirty aircraft and crews ready to operate. The following day, 23 March, there was no flying at all, the day being fully occupied with marshalling the Stirlings and the Horsa gliders into their take-off positions for the following morning.

Apart from a slight mist, 24 March dawned to perfect weather conditions. Our first combination (Wing Commander Bunker) took off at 0630 hours, the rest of the squadron following in quick order. By this time, we and the glider pilots were well trained in the technique of towing, and take-off and forming up were performed almost without a hitch. However, there was a delay of several minutes when a Stirling lost an engine on take-off. The aircraft swung violently, collapsing its undercarriage and blocking the runway. The crew were, thankfully, unhurt, but the Stirling was a write-off. Soon after this, our own part in 'Varsity' came to a premature end when our starboard inner engine developed a fault. The oil pressure dropped alarmingly and the cylinder head temperature began to rise rapidly. I told Ikey that the engine would have to be shut down and feathered, and this was done. It was quite possible for a Stirling running on three engines to tow a glider, but we were on an operation, towing a glider loaded with troops on their way to battle, and our cautious pilot decided to abort the flight and return to base. And so I missed most of the last great airborne operation of the war, in which the RAF glider tug losses were minimal, being one Dakota, three Halifaxes and three Stirlings, one of the later being the take-off crash at Great Dunmow. The following day we stood by for a resupply drop, but this was not needed as the airborne and ground forces had linked up a few hours after the landings.

A few days later our crew was given a six-day pass, and I went to a YCL camp at Sarratt, in Hertfordshire. But even on leave, in the peaceful English countryside, it was not possible to escape war and death. We were playing football on the camp field when two American Dakota transport aircraft passed, overhead, flying in close formation. As we stopped to watch, the wing of one Dakota touched that of the other, which came completely off, causing the aircraft to fall out of the sky. The second Dakota seemed to continue normally for a few seconds, but then it turned over and plunged to the ground. I could see that there was no chance of anyone surviving this crash. We heard later that two pilots had taken about twenty women personnel of the United States Air Force up for a flight, and presumably had flown that close to each other to allow their passengers to see one another more clearly.

On a much happier note, it was on this leave that I first met my future wife, Elizabeth Griffin. Elizabeth (later Beth) had joined the Women's Land Army, and was billeted on a farm near Feckenham, in Worcestershire. During the following months we corresponded and our interest in each other deepened.

Back from leave, our crew's next operation was a paratroop drop into Holland. This was SAS Operation 'Amherst', mounted in support of the 1st Canadian Army in its advance across Holland. A force of forty-six Stirlings were involved, each carrying fifteen troops and four containers. Our squadron contributed eight aircraft, which were briefed to drop their troops and containers in the area of Assen.

On the night of the operation, the weather was generally poor. All of the drop zones were covered by low stratus, in places reaching up to 1,500 feet. With the aid of GEE fixes, the troops and containers were dropped 'blind' from above the stratus, the first time this technique had been used on operations or in training. We saw a small amount of flak from Ameland, but no other opposition. The operation was successful.

Supply drops into Holland and Norway continued almost to the end of the war, and towards the middle of April the squadron began to operate over Denmark as well. At the same time, we began to ferry supplies of 100-octane petrol to forward airfields on the Continent, including Germany itself. The usual load was seventeen panniers, each containing seven-gallon jerry cans. As the panniers could not be carried in the bomb bay, they were loaded in the rear fuselage, which shifted the aircraft's centre of gravity (CG), making take-off and landing more difficult. This was aggravated by the well-cratered state of the destination airfields,

Liberated POWs wait to embark for their return to England.
Photograph courtesy of the Imperial War Museum

all of this making these operations less than popular with us. The return flights, however, were taken up with the much more agreeable task of bringing home liberated prisoners of war. An airfield at Brussels (littered with destroyed tanks and other debris of war) was a collecting point for these men, and from there we flew them to Wing, in Buckinghamshire, To do this, we were allowed to go there direct by flying over London, until then something strictly forbidden. On one trip to Wing, loaded with Army personnel, we very nearly ran out of fuel when in the air – my fuel gauges were reading 'empty'. I informed Ikey of this and suggested that the airfield be asked for permission to fly straight in rather than do the normal circuit before landing. This was granted and, thankfully, we landed safely. A crash at this stage would have been a tragedy for those ex-POWs, looking forward to peace and reunion with their families (and for us, of course).

It was on one of these repatriation operations that we lost our commanding officer, Wing Commander Bunker. After disembarking his passengers at Odiham, in Hampshire, he took off to return to Great Dunmow, and shortly afterwards the aircraft's tail unit caught fire. The Stirling went out of control and crashed at Windlesham, in Surrey, killing all on board. A little less than three weeks later the European war came to an end.

On 'Victory in Europe' day (VE Day), most of the people on the airbase were given leave. I made a beeline for the railway station and made my way to Acton, to find that my brother George was also home. After a meal, George, my father and mother and I, made our way to the Railway Hotel public house to celebrate. There were two attractive girls in the pub, so I began a conversation with them. George soon joined in the chat. When the pub closed, the girls invited us to a street celebration in a nearby street. The inhabitants had lit a fire in the middle of the road and had dragged out a piano for entertainment. So we danced hand in hand around the fire, singing and drinking from the bottles bought at the pub. This evening will never be forgotten by us, as George later married one of these girls – Rosalind – and the other acted as bridesmaid at the wedding!

Norway Again

And so the European war ended, with an unconditional surrender by Hitler's successor, Grand-Admiral Karl Dönitz. However, Norway had still to be liberated, and it was not known whether the German forces there would accept the orders of Dönitz or carry out Hitler's 'no surrender' call. The country was to be occupied by elements of the 1st Airborne Division and our squadron, with others, was to transport them there. We therefore loaded our aircraft with members of the 21st Independent Para Company (an elite force) and set off for Norway and the airfield of Gardermoen, located on a height above the capital, Oslo. We found the weather bad over the North Sea, but we carried on and landed safely, with the paratroops armed and ready. As soon as the aircraft rolled to a stop and I had opened the door, they jumped out and raced to the airfield buildings, ready for combat. Fortunately, the Germans had accepted the surrender order and there was no problem. So we too left the aircraft and wandered over to the buildings. I never saw a single German there. After a while, we left the paras and flew back to our base at Dunmow.

Two days later, we again went to Gardermoen, this time carrying supplies. The sea crossing was interrupted for the squadrons involved by having to conduct a square search of an area of sea, where two our squadron's aircraft were believed to have ditched two days before. We carried out our part of the search, myself combing the sea from the astrodome as we circled, but we saw nothing. Our search completed, we continued on to Gardermoen. We later heard that one of our aircraft had crashed, without survivors, north of Oslo. My friend, 'Fingers' Alderson, was one of the dead. Also on board, acting as second pilot, was the Air Officer Commanding 38 Group, Air Vice-Marshall J P Scarlett-Streatfield. Our other aircraft had ditched in a Swedish lake, without serious injury to the crew, but four of the troops being carried were killed.

German troops marching at Gardermoen.

Rouble note, given to me by an
ex-Russian POW at Oslo train station.

Our third trip to Gardermoen brought about a two-night stay, due to bad weather, so a group of us decided to make our way down to Oslo. We found the road and started to walk down it. Soon, we heard the sound of a truck behind us, so we gathered across the road, to see a German vehicle, fuelled by a gas bag on its top, coming towards us. Waving our guns, we forced it to stop and, despite the driver's grumbles, made him drive us into Oslo, one of us sitting in the driver's cab with a pistol trained on him!

In Oslo, having been given military money, we all piled into a restaurant – quite an experience, as the meal was very basic and primitive. We then began to stroll through the city, followed by a number of admiring young girls. Also wandering around aimlessly were a number of Russian ex-POWs, whom the British forces had liberated. I was able to have some conversation with them, using the Norwegian girls as interpreters. These girls were wonderful linguists. In addition to their own language, they could speak the German they'd learned during the occupation, and they could also speak enough English and Russian to interpret for us. I still have the addresses of some of these Russians, given then, although I had no reply to my letters to them. Finally, we made our way to the station to train back to Gardermoen – to find that the first train to there was not leaving until the following morning! However, after speaking to the stationmaster, we were given permission to sleep on benches in a waiting room.

The next morning we queued at the ticket office, and I was approached by a young Russian ex-POW, who fully intended to buy a ticket back to Russia! He had seen, and wanted, a hammer and sickle star badge which I always wore – illegally – on my uniform. I told him, 'No, me a communist,' pointing to myself. He then brought out a rouble note with a picture of Lenin on it. At this, I pointed to the picture, gave the thumbs up sign, and accepted the trade. I still have the rouble note.

So we trained and bussed back to Gardermoen, a small settlement which looked rather like a town of the American West, with raised wooden sidewalks and wooden buildings, the roadway not being made up. We walked back to the airfield, to find that an amount of supplies had been dropped by parachute, and that there were a number of silk chutes lying about. We grabbed these and cut them up to make knickers for our ladies. I then strolled over to a Junkers Ju 88, climbed in, and managed to remove an instrument for a souvenir. After this, I rejoined my crew, and we flew back to Dunmow. This ended my experience of Norway.

Our squadron was now converting to Halifaxes, and in the middle of May we began the disposal of our Stirlings. They were flown, in batches, to Magheraberry, near Lisburn, in County Antrim, for storage and eventual scrapping. It is a sad fact that not one Stirling was saved for the museums, or to give pleasure to people at an air display in the future. Our crew took its turn in this melancholy task. On the way in across the coast of Northern Ireland, we could see the Mountains of Mourne, but Ireland was a washout, with rain, and we were glad to fly back in a Dakota. I preferred four-engined aircraft!

During this period immediately after the war, members of the squadron were allowed to visit Coventry, to see for ourselves the devastation there. Landing at a nearby 'drome, we were bussed to the city and allowed to wander around among the devastated buildings and to see the cathedral, left a dismal ruin. Another time, our crew was given the chance to see a little of what was left of Germany, after the devastation wrought by the RAF and the Americans. My main memory of this was of the sight when we flew close to Hanover. The centre of the city had literally disappeared, turned to rubble. Around the centre was a ring of largely untouched suburban buildings. On a another flight, we saw similar devastation when flying over the German railway centre of Hamm. Germany had certainly reaped the whirlwind.

New Aircraft, New Crew, New Wife

This was my last big trip with my wartime crew for, soon after, came a flurry of postings out, including a mass exchange of personnel with 620 Squadron. Our crew broke up. Our two Aussies, Ikey and Ross, went back to Australia. A quote from the book, *Schindler's List*, by Thomas Keneally, illustrates the contribution made by the Australians.

> When he [Schindler] got back [to Cracow] he found that an Allied bomber, shot down by a Luftwaffe fighter, had crashed on the two end barracks in the backyard prison. Its blackened fuselage sat crookedly across the wreckage of the flattened huts ... a small squad of prisoners ... had seen it come down, flaming ... The bomber was a Stirling and the men were Australian. One, who was holding the charred remnants of an English Bible, must have crashed with it in his hand. Two others had parachuted in the suburbs. One had been found, dead of wounds, in his harness. The partisans had got to the other one first and were hiding him somewhere. What these Australians had been doing was dropping supplies to the partisans in the primeval forest east of Cracow. ... If Oskar had needed some sort of confirmation, this was it. That men should come all this way from unimaginable little towns in Australia to hasten the end in Cracow.

As for the rest of our crew, my friend Bob Sutton was posted out to 298 Squadron, then in India. Arthur Batten, our air gunner, remained with 190 Squadron. Where Ron Bradbury, our wireless operator and now a pilot officer, went or what became of him, I do not know. It speaks much for the sense of transience and change that we had become accustomed to accept, that we took this parting of the ways quite calmly and matter of course.

I myself was posted in mid-July to the Operational & Refresher Training Unit at Matching, in Essex. This mainly for

With some of my new mates, by a Halifax 111 aircraft.
Myself, C W Chapman, 'Titch' Walters, E Smith and D Macintyre.

The crew again, with an addition.
K C Pettit; D Macintyre; C W Chapman; myself and 'Titch' Walters.

re-crewing, as the Halifax IIIs operated by ORTU were powered by the same Bristol Hercules engines that I was familiar with. I was introduced to my new crew. The pilot was Squadron Leader D MacIntyre, whom the crew soon came to know as 'Mac'. The other crew members were: Flight Sergeant Hill (second pilot), Pilot Officer Smith ('Smithy' – navigator), Flight Sergeant Chapman (bomb aimer), Pilot Officer Flynn (wireless operator), Flight Sergeant 'Titch' Walters (air gunner) and myself, Flight Sergeant Mitchell (flight engineer). Titch and I struck up a friendship, but the others I met only when we were flying or at meals in the mess etc. Towards the end of July we were posted to 644 Squadron, stationed at Tarrant Rushton, from where I had taken off for my very first operation.

In the first week of August, we took part in a troop-drooping exercise in Yorkshire. It was on the return flight from this exercise that our wireless operator heard the news that a new type of bomb – atomic – had been dropped on Japan. I realised then that the whole concept of warfare had changed for ever. This was followed a few days later by a second atomic bomb, and by Russia's declaration of war on Japan, which surrendered less than a week later. The Second World War was finally over.

Later that month of August, we took part in Operation 'Hellas' 2, which involved ferrying Greek 'displaced persons' back to their homeland. The operation was spread over four days. The first leg of the flight took us to Brussels, where we stayed overnight and collected our passengers. Taking off early the following morning, we flew to Foggia (Italy), where we refuelled before continuing to Athens. This we reached after flying down the length of the Corinth Canal, the sides of it level with the wings of our aircraft. We stayed for two nights and were fortunate enough to be billeted by the Aegean Sea, a marvellously clear sea, in which we swam, looking at the rocks below. Driving into Athens, we noticed people apparently living in slit trench-type hovels by the side of the road. I saw the Acropolis, high on its hill, while driving into town. Athens seemed untouched, and quite a busy city. We returned to England by way of Foggia, and after stopping off at Merryfield, in Somerset, returned to Tarrant Rushton.

*The Corinth Canal, which crosses the Corinth Isthmus, linking the Gulf of Cornith
and the Ionian Sea with the Saronic Gulf and the Aegean Sea.*

Piraeus, sea port for Athens.

It was during this spring and summer that I was courting my future wife, Elizabeth. This was done mainly by letter, although we did meet occasionally when our leaves coincided. On one leave I was able to meet her in Birmingham for a couple of days and then take her back to Feckenham, near where she was billeted. We also had one wonderful leave at home, from where we made our way back to Sarratt, where we had first met. It was there that I asked Elizabeth (Beth, by then) to become my wife, and asked her to arrange the wedding. And so I received a letter from her, asking me to get a leave on Saturday, 1 September, to meet her at her home and be married at Burnt Oak Marriage Registry Office in Middlesex. I promptly obtained a forty-eight-hour pass for that weekend. But, when I arrived at her house in Kingsbury, I learned that the wedding could not take place until Monday, 3 September. At this, I immediately telegraphed Squadron Leader MacIntyre, my superior and pilot, to ask for an extension of leave. The permission arrived by telegram on the Sunday.

Finally, on the Monday, Elizabeth and I, her mother and mine, her sister Moira, brother David and my brother George – on leave from the Marines – drove to the Registry Office and were married. We then had the best part of a week to honeymoon at Kingsbury and Acton. At the end of this period, Elizabeth went back to her farm, but I stayed on leave until my money ran out! When I eventually arrived back at my station, about three weeks later, I found that my Squadron Leader and pilot, Mac, had hardly missed me, so carefree and laid-back was he. 'Where have you been?' he asked.

'Waiting for you to recall me!' I answered. And that was the end of that.

No. 644 Squadron badge: in front of an increscent, a Pegasus rampant.

Motto: 'Dentes draconis serimus' ('We sow dragon's teeth).

Authority: King George VI, February 1945.

Origin: The Pegasus symbolises the squadron's task of carrying air-borne troops into battle. The increscent indicates night operations, when arms and supplies were dropped to the resistance groups in enemy-occupied France. The motto was inspired by the ancient Greek myth of the hero Cadmus, who killed a great dragon that was guarding the well of Ares. At the bidding of the goddess Athena, Cadmus sowed the soil with the dragon's teeth, whereupon armed men sprang up out of the ground, clashing their weapons together.

Photograph courtesy of the Imperial War Museum, London

Palestine

A few days after my return, we flew to Prague with a load of Czech State gold, which had earlier been sent to Britain for safety. We flew over Prague first, for a look, then landed at Prague Airport, where the gold, in wooden boxes, was accepted by the authorities. We did not get near to any of the airport buildings, but I did at least see one Russian officer there, looking resplendent in his best uniform! Then back to England, after little more than two hours on Czech territory and no refuelling, which left me very short again on the return at night – with no parachute, my diary tells me. Nasty. We flew to Prague again that week, with a further cargo of gold. This time, I was able to have a talk with an official of the National Bank of Czechoslovakia, who spoke English well. The next week, Prague yet again, this time to see a number of ex-slave girls, who were on their way home.

The squadron had been gradually re-equipping with tropicalised Halifaxes and finally, after a number of last leaves, orders came for us to move to Palestine. We therefore packed and waited, then were briefed and began the move, without gliders this time. I was now quite familiar with the Halifax (remember, the engines were the same four reliable Hercules radials that I was well used to), although I never did properly learn the fuel quantities in each tank in the wings. I merely carried a diagram in my tool bag which gave that information. And so we flew across France to the Mediterranean and across to Tunisia, landing at El Aouina, near Tunis. After a meal and a wash and brush up, we piled onto a lorry and drove into Tunis, to hit the nearest café in the centre. The air was warm and balmy and the sky was clear and blue to welcome us to Africa. There were a number of locals in the café and we seemed to be accepted as something normal by them, especially as we all behaved ourselves. A couple of then were Jewish and claimed that they were communists, but this was doubtful. After a few wines and some chat, we strolled back to the

Myself at the billet door in Qastina.

lorry and, after queuing to relieve ourselves against the rear offside wheel – as per instructions – drove back to the airfield and our billets for the night.

The next morning saw us taking off on an easterly course over the Atlas Mountains, which stretched magnificently far below us, in an arid landscape. Crossing the coast, we flew across the Mediterranean to Palestine, a bright patchwork of greens and browns, landing at the RAF base at Qastina (El Qastine), set in flat land below hills. A truck met us there and carried us to our respective messes, the Sergeants' Mess being a large permanent building (in England we had Nissen huts for accommodation and Messing), with marble-topped tables to eat on, sitting on stone benches, warm to the touch. After a good meal, we were shown to our billets. Again, these were sturdy permanent stone and concrete huts.

Life at Qastina soon settled into a pattern. The flight buildings and the aircraft were a good ten minutes' truck drive away. Much of our time was spent in the accommodation and administration areas, reading, eating and visiting the camp cinema, with its British and American films subtitled in French, which helped me to easily learn to read the language. It was a new experience to be continually bathed in bright sunlight and to wear shorts, with long trousers worn only in the evenings against the insects and the coolness.

In the course of my flying duties, I saw much of Palestine from the air. Our early flights were over the local countryside, on our customary air tests, glider tows and para drops with the 6th Airborne Division, who were in Palestine with us and were billeted near to our airfield. One night flight was memorable, as we flew over a brightly lit Tel Aviv, the first lighted town that I had ever seen from the air.

Soon it was Christmas 1945, and we were treated to a fine three-course Christmas dinner, served in style by our Arab waiters in the mess. Adjoining the dining room was a large recreational area, fitted with comfortable easy chairs and tables for drinks and cards etc., together with a drinks bar. We were treated to an entertainment on that occasion. At other times, someone would occasionally set a housey housey (bingo or tombola) game going there for us non-comms.

'Fighter Afield' practise with a Mustang fighter, over Palestine.

View from the rear of the Halifax, showing the towed Horsa glider.

I had made a good friend of one of my fellow flight engineers, Steve Lyden, and a great deal of my leisure time was spent in his company.

Our normal day saw us being driven down to the 'flights' after breakfast and a possible flight, with or without a glider. Then, back to the mess for lunch, following which we usually repaired to our huts to sunbathe and read – unless a trip to Tel Aviv, twenty mils away, for the cafés or cinema, or to the sea for a swim near the village of Majdal, had been laid on. There were also buses to Tel Aviv which could be taken. The road out of the camp passed through an orange grove. On the way back into camp, I would reach a hand through the separating wire and steal a Jaffa or two.

After the evening meal we might stroll up to the camp cinema, where sometimes a concert of sorts would be held. I also attended a music circle, to listen to classical music. But a new interest was being organised for those who wished to take part, Educational and Vocational Training (EVT), at a lecture block. I entered classes for English and Mathematics, and had the nerve to offer to teach economics one evening a week! It turned out to be good practise for my future career as a schoolteacher.

Some of our flights were very interesting, as was the one across Palestine to the Red Sea, flying mainly over desert and seeing below the occasional Arab tented settlement. From the air, the RAF station of Aqaba, on the Gulf of Aqaba, appeared terribly isolated. I thank my stars that I was not stationed there! On that trip we lost an escape hatch and a window, blown out and away...

Myself at a café, on the Tel Aviv front, with two friends and 'Titch'.

A friend, 'Titch' and myself on a railing by the Mediterranean Sea.

Back to Blighty, via Malta

Far more interesting to us was a mail run flight back to England. We began by flying to Almaza, in Egypt, and spending the evening in Heliopolis, near Cairo. Back to the airfield the following day for the nest leg of our flight, which was across the Med to the RAF station of Luqa, on the island of Malta. Here, after a clean-up and some food, some of us went down to Valletta. The truck dropped us at Floriana, an extension of Valletta up from the harbour. In the company of three or four other aircrew, I walked downhill to and through Valletta. My most vivid memory is of narrow roadways with tall buildings on either side, a great deal of bomb damage, but clear streets, and statues of Christ or Mary high up at the corner of every street. We eventually made our way to a street called, we understood, The Gut, with many cafés and bars in it (one of us must have known the city). After wandering around this very steep road, we entered one of the cafés and made our way upstairs to the bar, crowded with sailors and women. We bought wine and sat down to chat with two or three women sitting there. I got into conversation with one of them who was somewhat younger and better looking than the others. It gradually dawned on me, as I continued the conversation, that all the women were prostitutes. Mine told me that she was the breadwinner of her family, and I had no reason to doubt her. Due to the presence of the Navy and the Grand Harbour, prostitution seemed to be one of the main industries of Valletta.

As the evening advanced and the drinks were sunk, the sailors in the bar became more noisy and excited. The women played up to them and the scene became wilder. I will not elaborate on this, but it finally became too much for us staid RAF men, and we left, to walk back to where our truck was waiting far us. We stayed in Malta for four days, visiting Floriana and Valletta a number of tines, to wander round the streets, visit the cinema and eat in the

NAAFI there. What we saw of the countryside on the way to town seemed rocky and infertile, a home for sheep and goats.

Leaving the island, we then flew back to England, landing at Earls Colne airfield in Essex. Then, for me, it was on to Acton, where I was reunited with my parents. I was allowed a long leave at home, provided that I phoned regularly to keep in touch. Most of the time was spent with Beth, at her home, but I was also able to spend time with my parents, brother George and his girl, Rosalind. But, good tines coming to an end, I was recalled after a week, and flew back to Palestine and Qastina, via Luqa.

Attacked!

One evening, a fortnight later, our base was attacked by Jewish resistance forces. There were a number of resistance/liberation/terrorist organisations (depending on your viewpoint) operating in Palestine at this time. We were alerted to this attack by the sound of machine-gun fire. I strapped on my revolver and made my way to the Sergeants' Mess as a rallying point. The mess lighting was blazing away merrily through windows that weren't blacked out, so I suggested that we stand in the dark, rather than become easy targets. The lighting was duly doused and we stood by awaiting orders. These finally came, telling us that the attack was over and we could return to our billets. The next day, we learned that no one of ours had been killed, but three of our Halifaxes had been completely burned out and eight others wrecked and damaged beyond repair. One of the attackers had been killed. Ironically, many of these Jews had been trained in sabotage work during the war – by the British!

A few days later, we abandoned Qastina and moved down to the RAF base at Bilbeis, in Egypt. I found it most strange, but interesting, to take the journey by train, in charge of a group of airmen. Bilbeis was set in the desert, near to the Sweetwater Canal – a misnomer if ever there was one. We were told that this canal was so filthy that if a serviceman fell in he would have to be pumped full with injections! Instead of purpose-built huts, I found myself living in a tent, in searing heat. The very first day, I managed to burn my tent down, with a carelessly discarded cigarette. The tent went up like a bomb, giving us barely time to get out of it. My clothes and belongings in the tent went up too, and I had to be issued with new kit. Not only was there heat to contend with on this station, but one day a wind sprang up and we found ourselves in the middle of a sandstorm. For much of the day, we sheltered and cowered in our tent, but it was obviously necessary to visit the mess for our meals and the loos, and for that we had to brave the storm.

A carpenter at work in Baghdad. Notice the open front; the carpenter sold his wares as he made them.

As soon as I left the tent my eyes, ears and all parts were hit by flying sand, and it was difficult to glimpse the way ahead. It seemed to take an age to reach the mess building, and once there I was in no hurry to return to the tent!

We aircrew were given a rota of nights when, for security reasons, we had to sleep in our aircraft, with a ground airman on guard outside each plane. What would happen to us if these aircraft were attacked while we were asleep, we never did discover! The defences at Qastina were being strengthened and we made a number of visits there during this period, using it as a base to fly to Nicosia, in Cyprus, and to other destinations, such as Habbaniya, in Iraq. On one such flight, we had to fly a stick of paratroops to a point near Baghdad, where they were to jump, as an exercise. Tragically, as we later heard, some of them dropped into the Tigris and were drowned.

On another occasion, while staying at the RAF airbase at Habbaniya, we drew lots for a trip by truck, across a barren landscape, to Baghdad. Sadly, on the way our truck was involved in an accident, and one of us received back injuries, from which he slowly died on the floor of the stationary truck. We others were ordered to wait at the roadside. After the police and the ambulance (in that order) had reached us and taken the body, the truck continued into Baghdad, crossing the Tigris on the way. We were given a few hours to wander round, finding the place very primitive, with unmade roads and open-fronted shops, where Arabs were working at making shoes, pots etc. Women in the streets were dressed in black from head to foot with apertures for their eyes, a depressing sight to our Western eyes. I bought a souvenir or two, and then made my way back to the truck and thence back to Habbaniya, to fly back to Bilbeis. The death of our comrade preyed on my mind, and shortly after I wrote a poem about it.

The Accident

His name came first from out the hat –
He smiled and said,
'Why, I at least shall surely see
Baghdad.'

But, as he spoke, Death left Baghdad
To meet us on that dusty road
And embraced him, he who with us
Was laughing in the truck.

Our names, too, came from the hat…?
But fate, that day
Wore a black hat
From which his name came singly.

His epitaph?
What else but that:
His name came first
From out the hat.

Incidentally, I wrote a number of poems while I was abroad, separated from my wife and family; with much time on my hands and reading poetry myself, I was in the mood to do so.

Being based quite near to Cairo, a group of us did have the chance to visit the city and the nearby Pyramids and the Sphinx. I climbed to the top of the largest, Cheops' Pyramid (my brother George told me that he had carved his name there and mine, as have many others) and, entering it, climbed the Grand Staircase, to visit the tomb room at its heart. The Sphinx, I found, was a temple, entered between its front legs. A camel ride completed the day. The next day saw us taking an interesting flight down the Suez Canal to the RAF station at Kabritt.

The bridge over the Tigris, near Baghdad.

Street scene in Baghdad, with the mosque in the background.

A fortnight later, we packed and left Bilbeis to return thankfully to a fortified and well-guarded Qastina. I had now been promoted to Warrant Officer, and along with my promotion came extra duties, one of which was to be the NCO in charge of a night guard. This was a strange duty for a member of an aircrew, as marching a squad of men to a guard post was hardly what I had been trained to do! Neither was leaving my bed in a guard hut every two hours, to walk round a large area to ensure that the airmen on guard at points (who were relieved at intervals) were still awake and vigilant. Occasionally one was not, as the airmen were not accustomed to this duty after a full day's work, and objected to it strongly. Another unusual duty was to attend the airmen's mess at meal times, to wander around and ask, 'Any complaints?' I also had to visit the camp cells, to ensure that the prisoners were being treated properly. I still remember the prisoner whom I met on one of these visits – a brawny, sullen, monosyllabic paratrooper, who looked at me with a very jaundiced eye when I asked him if he had any complaints! On another night guard, I was in charge of a group of men and a large searchlight, which was set on a hill dominating an area of countryside. This was fun, as I could have it directed to where I wished over this area. I doubt if the farmers there enjoyed having their farm buildings bathed in intense light during the night hours, however.

Our airfield was not attacked again, but the Jewish resistance/terrorists were not idle, for they machine-gunned a group of 6th Airborne men coming out of a café, killing seven of them. Who did this we never learned, for there were a number of organisations fighting the British. The Haganah was the main liberation army, but there were other groupings, such as the Irgun Zwei Leumi and the so-called 'Stern Gang', the latter a very unpleasant crew. The response of our paras to the Tel Aviv affair was to go to the nearby Jewish village and beat up the inhabitants. How to win friends and influence people!

Now back at Qastina, I resumed my Educational and Vocational Studies and the giving of lectures in economics, which I had studied while in the YCL. I found, to my surprise, that I was to be paid for these lectures. I had heard of the possibility of winning an ex-serviceman's grant to attend teacher training college, and so I determined to get on such a course when I left the RAF. In study, I found the mastering of English, and English grammar came easily, but mathematics, especially geometry, I found exceedingly difficult, if not impossible. I also read much classical literature and poetry, being especially fond of Shelley's 'Ozymandias'. It was in this period of my time at Qastina that I was asked to go to Jerusalem, to the YCA building there, to be interviewed by people from the Ministry of Education, on my application for ex-serviceman's grant to attend a teacher training college, upon my release from the RAF. The interview was exclusively oral. They asked me what my interests were, and when I mentioned poetry I was asked to recite a poem. Thankfully, by this time I had learned 'Ozymandias' right through, and was able to recite it quite satisfactorily. Two days after this interview, I learned that my application had been successful. I had won a grant to college!

I had been keeping myself very fit since arriving at Qastina, but now had a shock – I caught sandfly fever! The symptoms were a temperature and very severe diarrhoea, which put me in the station hospital, where I spent my time crouched over a pot with my trousers down. This could not have happened at a worse time, as the squadron put on a flight to Khartoum, which I would loved to have visited. However, I was fit enough later to be part of the ceremonial fly-past over Jerusalem in honour of the King's birthday.

While in the Middle East, I had been writing regularly to my new wife, who was now having our baby and living with my parents, as her mother had moved to a caravan in the village of Whipsnade, in Bedfordshire. In June came a telegram from my mother, to tell me that my son Steven had been born. He was named after my closest friend on the squadron. Letters from Beth and my mother followed, confirming the birth, with congratulations. I was now a father! At this time I also learned that a Mention in Despatches in my name had been published in the London *Gazette*, presumably because I had managed to survive the Arnhem debacle.

By the KING'S Order the name of
Flight Sergeant M. Mitchell.
Royal Air Force Volunteer Reserve.
was published in the London Gazette on
1 January 1946.
as mentioned in a Despatch for distinguished service.
I am charged to record
His Majesty's high appreciation.

Secretary of State for Air

I am mentioned in the Despatches.

Early the following month, on a Monday night, I had a night guard duty. The next day saw the stressful Civil Service examination in English and Maths that I had been studying for. The following day our crew took off on a mail run to England. After dropping in at Kasfareet (Egypt), we landed at Almaza and made our way to a Cairo hotel (Shepherds?), to stay for the night. However, the crew were keen to press on home, so after a meal we left the hotel for the airfield and took off for a night flight to Italy, landing at Castel Benito. After breakfast and refuelling, we took off for Tarrant Rushton and England. By this time I was so tired that, at one stage, I fell asleep standing up by my instruments in the aircraft. Coming to with a start, I hurriedly checked that all was well with my engines.

We landed in the late afternoon, and then it was by train to London and bus to Acton, arriving dead beat in the late evening, having to carry two large cases from the bus stop uphill to my home. It was grand to see my parents and my wife and to see my child, Steven, for the very first time, but I was overwrought and soon went to bed. However, I found it impossible to get to sleep. The doctor, called in the early hours of the following night, diagnosed nervous exhaustion, prescribed drugs and ordered rest. This rest, on doctor's orders, stretched out to over four weeks, by which time my aircraft and crew had long gone back to Palestine. I was finally allowed to leave, and was given a lift back as a supplementary crew member in an aircraft leaving from Pershore, in Worcestershire. Arriving back at Qastina, I found that I was temporarily grounded. This grounding became permanent, as I was parted from my crew and posted to Aqir and then to Almaza, prior to demobilisation.

Egypt and Demob!

Almaza proved to be a very happy station for me. It was possible to walk to a bus stop and drive into Cairo, and I made a number of visits there. Sometimes it would be to an open-air cinema, which showed British and American films (with French subtitles), shown on a screen which sometimes fluttered in the breeze. The show always ended with the playing of the Egyptian National Anthem, to which we British sang, sotto voce, '*Staniswire** *King Farouk, Hang your bollocks on a hook, Staniswire pull your wire, You're a liar, King Farouk!*' – showing that the RAF had somewhat increased my vocabulary. I also shopped and wandered around Cairo, whose citizens seemed reasonably friendly, especially when we were spending our money there!

At Almaza, I was reunited with my very good friend, Steve Lyden. He had been the Three 'A's boxing champion of Newcastle. Wishing to get back into training he needed a sparring partner – yours truly. And so, under his instruction, I learned to be a boxer, a southpaw, as I am left-handed. With the very good food of the camp and the regular exercise – we started the day with a run round the perimeter track, which skirted the landing ground, and then ducked under ropes tied to four poles banged into the ground – and the boxing, I became fitter than I have ever been, before or since.

As my official work, I had been placed in charge of a Transport Office, Air Movements, to log arrivals and departures etc. One of my assistants was a young German POW from the desert campaign. A confident, perhaps cocky individual, he was convinced of the correctness of Germany's actions and of the greatness of Hitler. Having seen his bombed and ruined country, I tried to tell of what he would meet when he returned home, but he would have none of it – it was purely British propaganda and lies.

* Staniswire was a word invented by the lads to rhyme with 'wire'.

Egypt. The Spinx and the Pyramids.

Myself on Cheops, the pyramid, with a friend.

I now experienced official duplicity. I was inveigled into accepting a new designation as a Physical Training Instructor (PTI), thinking that it would help in my new career as a teacher. When I had agreed to this change, I found myself reduced to the rank of Sergeant. I had also been given certain documents relevant to my discharge, including a paybook containing a reference – written by an officer who had never seen me! I was forthwith posted to Kasfareet, near the Bitter Lakes, where I could see a section of the Suez Canal and the ships passing through. The base, standing in the desert, was very basic: tents, a mess, ablutions, an airfield and a view of the lakes. Half of the time I was there I suffered stomach upsets etc., due to the change of food – and probably water – and I was very glad when the day came to pack my kitbag and leave. A week in that place was more than enough! So I went by truck along a road paralleling the Suez Canal and through the desert to Port Said and a ship, a small vessel called the *Ortuna*. Arriving on board, I realised keenly why I had been conned into relinquishing my warrant officer status, for we sergeants were directed into the bowels of the ship, with little space for our belongings and a hammock to sleep in. This appliance was new to me, and did not improve my sleep while on board. A colleague who had resisted the blandishments of the RAF and had kept his warrant officer's crown, had a cabin up near the deck, and individual food. Our food was collected in bulk by us from the galley, then taken down to be shared out and eaten. It was just about edible.

And so we set sail, on a calm and bright Mediterranean, for three days of absolute boredom, relieved for me only by reading, until we reached the Grand Harbour of Malta, where we stayed (on board) overnight. Then on our way again, the weather turning cold and rainy. The 'heads' (latrines) were disgusting, with four or five inches of sea water and urine sloshing around over our shoes and smelling abominably. Passing Pantelleria, Sardinia and Corsica, we arrived three days later at Toulon. After disembarking, we were driven to another primitive transit camp, and to a train the following clay, for an interesting ride through France to Calais. There, after dumping our gear, we were allowed out. I made my way into town and to the Communist Party premises, where I met the French communists, including the Mayor of Calais.

A storm in the Channel had prevented the ferries from sailing for the previous three days, I was told, but the weather improved a little and we sailed for Dover the next day. The ship pitched and rolled and nearly all of the passengers were seasick – not I, possibly due to my flight experience. However, Dover soon hove into view, and then it was by train to London, and home!

Unfortunately, it was but a flying visit, with just enough time to see my parents and brother George, by now demobbed. Five hours later, near to midnight, I left for RAF Kirkham, arriving there at six the following morning. After a sleep, I gave in most of my kit (hanging on to as much as I thought that I could get away with) and took an early bed. Next day, I was given 'civvy' clothes – rather basic – issued with further documents, such as an employment book, and was officially demobilised. I then left Kirkham, on six weeks' demob leave from the RAF with a £130 parting gratuity, and made my way, via Luton, to Whipsnade. Here, my wife, Beth, and my son, Steven, were now living with her mother, Lydia, her sister, Moira and brother, David – all in a horse-drawn-type caravan in a snow-covered farmer's field! So, temporarily, I moved in as well! Or rather, I commuted between there and Acton, hoping to find a place for us in my home town. I registered my name with the town hall for a council home, and eventually found the empty downstairs floor of a house to move into (without the knowledge of the owner!) with my new family.

A New Life

Work was difficult to find, as the winter of 1946–47 proved to be a bitter one. There was very little coal, and factories had closed down, due to the shortage of fuel and electricity. I could not find work in such conditions, and was forced to live on my leave money and later, my gratuity. During this winter many rural areas were completely cut off by snow. Aircraft of my recent squadron (now back in England and based at Fairford) were used to drop food and other supplies to isolated villages. On 13 February 1947, my onetime crew, including Squadron MacIntyre and the flight engineer who had replaced me, were performing this function in the hilly northern part of Staffordshire. They had been briefed for a supply drop at the village of Butterton, which required a low-level approach to the snow-covered drop zone, this being marked by the villagers with soot crosses. Sadly, it appears that Mac misread the contours, probably due to the snow covering, and failed to notice a rise in the ground. The Halifax ploughed into high ground on Grindon Moor, some eight miles east of Leek, and near Butterton, killing all on board. Those killed were: Sqn Ldr D MacIntyre (pilot); Flt Lt E Smith (navigator); Sig E C Pettit (wireless operator); Nav G W Chapman (bomb aimer); U S Kearns (flight engineer); Sgt W Sherry (Glider Pilot Regiment); Mr Saville (*Daily Herald*) and Mr Reardon (Keystone Press Agency). While in Palestine, Mac had offered to get me a commission if I would stay in the RAF as an engineer with him and the crew but, now having a wife and child in England, and my promise of a teacher college training grant, I declined the offer. Had I accepted I would, presumably, have been in that aircraft.

This, then, was my terrible farewell to the RAF. When the winter's grip finally broke and factories resumed production, I was fortunate enough to win a position as Technical Author at the Acton factory of D Napier and Son (who had been my first employer, in 1936), helping to write the technical manual for the Napier Sabre in-line sleeve-valve aero engine.

Postscript

I suppose that it could be said that I had a 'good' war. I was well paid, well fed and slept in white sheets. I had regular leave to visit home, and most of the time I was in no danger. When I was, I was lucky, and lucky to have a cautious pilot and an experienced crew. However, luck it was, as the gravestones of Wing Commander Harrison and Squadron Leader Gilliard, among others of my squadron in the Military Cemetery at Oosterbeek, can testify.

War is not an adventure, and I wince when I see the adverts for young men to 'Join up and become men'. After the end of the war in Europe, we were returning from a paratroop-dropping exercise in Yorkshire when our wireless operator received a message, which he passed on to us. An atom bomb had been dropped on a city in Japan. Despite our ignorance of the power of that bomb, we realised that warfare had taken on a new, far more horrific dimension. Later, we learned that it also meant we would not be called to fight in the Far East, to which we had resigned ourselves.

I believed, and still believe, that World War Two was a just war. Fascism/Nazism had to be defeated. It was, but only partly, for neo-Nazism, revanchism and racism still threaten and corrupt our lives. The struggle goes on.

In 1950, I was on the streets and knocking on doors with the Stockholm Appeal against nuclear weapons. I have been a member of the Campaign for Nuclear Disarmament (CND) from its inception, and am still a member, and a member also of the Ex-Servicemen's CND. The struggle goes on.

A number of years after the war, I was introduced to a member of the Parachute Regiment Association, who invited me to a meeting of the Luton Branch of that Association. They were engaged in organising a coach trip to Arnhem. I was kindly invited to join them and, though not a 'para', I willingly agreed to do so.

F/L Lord's gravestone, Oosterbeek Military Cemetery.

Squadron Leader of 'B' Flight, 190 Squadron, L P Gilliard DFC's gravestone, Oosterbeek Military Cemetery.

Wing Commander W C Harrison's gravestone at Oosterbeek Military Cemetery.

While there I shared a room with two paras and was further invited to join them in their trips around Arnhem, getting to know the city, which I had never seen from the ground! A trip was also made to Oosterbeek, including a visit to the military museum, founded in the Hartenstein Hotel, which had been the headquarters of the First Parachute Division, under General Urquart, during the battle. I was also taken to the Military Cemetery at Oosterbeek, where those who fell are buried – including Flight Lieutenant D S A Lord, VC, DFC; my Squadron Leader, L P Gilliard, and 190's Wing Commander, G F Harrison.

The trip ended with a social, where I was asked to speak of my own experiences above Arnhem. These paras were magnificent lads and I accepted an invitation to join their Arnhem Veterans' Club. I have been a member ever since and have enjoyed the hospitality of the people of Arnhem, freely given. I have made lifelong friends there and at Oosterbeek.

Note

As I have restricted myself to my personal experiences, I have not included a bibliography. However, I recommend the reading of the excellent book, *Arnhem, the Battle Remembered*, by Hobert Jackson, who gives an exhaustive account. Also, the operational details are culled from the *Operations Record Book* for 190 Squadron, held by the National Archives at Kew under references Air 27/1154 and 2579, which repay careful study.

Myself at the Oosterbeek Cemetery, with a wreath, in 1994.

Prince Charles at Oosterbeek Cemetery, 1994.

Appendices

The following research was undertaken by Mr Tony Mawby.

Appendix 1

Operations: The Isaacson Crew

——28/29.04.44

SOE operation. 2310–0516 hrs.
Stirling IV, LJ818 'X'.

Operated from Tarrant Rushton. Supply drop in France, near the Swiss border. Successful. Twenty-four containers dropped. Other three squadron aircraft operating received no reception signals – forced to bring back their loads.

——06.06.44

Operation 'Mallard'. 1950–2340 hrs
Stirling IV, LJ881 'Z'.

Towed Horsa (Chalk no. 215) to LZ 'W', between Ouistreham and Caen. Horsa flown by Staff Sgt Bates and Sgt Johnstone. Carried one jeep, one trailer, one 75 mm gun and three troops. Successful. LZ recognised visually and by Eureka beacon. Glider seen to land ¾-mile NW of LZ. Nine containers dropped; all parachutes being seen to open.

Crossed in French coast:	2117 hrs at position: 49.18N 00.16W
Over LZ:	2118 hrs
Crossed out French coast:	2122 hrs at position: 49.17N 00.18W

2126 hrs – Halifax seen ditched off French coast in position 49.29N 00.16W. Launch seen heading towards spot.

Note: The ditched Halifax was LL407 of 298 Squadron, which had been hit by flak and ditched twelve miles off French coast. All of the crew were rescued.

——18.06.44

Operation 'Town Hall 8'. 2031–2300 hrs.
Stirling IV, LJ82O.

Supply drop in Normandy bridgehead. Successful.

——14/15.07.44

SOE Operation 'Stationer' 74. 2316–0512 hrs.
Stirling IV, LK4O5 'W'. 2nd pilot Flt Lt Mercer.

Supply drop over France. Unsuccessful. Incorrect reception signals at DZ. After three runs with same result returned to base without dropping.

Note: There is a possibility this DZ was 'trapped' with guns and searchlights. Such a trap was sprung on at least one other occasion, by a Stirling of 190 Squadron. It was lucky to escape.

——17/18.07.44

SAS operation 'Grog'. 2255–0224 hrs.
Stirling IV, LJ818 'X'.

Supply/paratroop drop in Lorient area of France. Successful. One of fifteen squadron aircraft, dropping a total of 338 containers, thirty-two panniers and thirteen SAS troops.

——20/21.07.44

SOE Operation. 2330–0240 hrs.
Stirling IV, LJ816.

Supply drop in France. Successful. Twenty-four containers dropped. Weather conditions very bad. Eighteen squadron aircraft operating.

——01/02.08.44

SOE Operation 'Donald'. 2223–0427 hrs.
Stirling IV, EF242 'Q'.

Supply drop in north Finistère region of France. Unsuccessful – no reception. Load brought back. Six squadron aircraft operating – four successful.

Note: 'Donald' was the cover name of an OSS group operating in Finistère.

——03/04.08.44

SAS Operation 'Moses'. 2207–0340 hrs.
Stirling IV, LJ83I.

Supply drop in the Vienne region of France. Successful. Ten squadron aircraft operating. Eight successful, dropping a total of 175 containers, twenty panniers and twenty-seven paratroops.

——25/26.08.44

SOE Operation. 2223–0623 hrs.
Stirling IV, LJ881 'Z'.

Supply drop in France. Successful – twenty-four containers dropped. Sixteen squadron aircraft operating. Bad weather conditions on return flight.

——26/27.08.44

SOE Operation. 2209–0455 hrs.
Stirling IV, LJ934 'Y'.

Supply drop in France. Successful. Eleven squadron aircraft operating – five successful. Bad weather.

——31.08.44

SOE Operation. 2313–0605 hrs.
Stirling IV, LJ832 'U'.

Supply drop in France. Unsuccessful. Unable to identify DZ due to low cloud. Load brought back. Eighteen squadron aircraft operating – nine successful.

——05/06.09.44

SOE Operation. 2122–0206 hrs.
Stirling IV, LJ982 'L9-N'.
2nd pilot Flt Sgt McGregor.

Supply drop in France. SAS troops also dropped. Successful.

——09/10.09.44

SOE Operation. 2110–0205 hrs.
Stirling IV, LJ936 'G5-N'.
2nd pilot Flt Sgt Wimms.

One of eleven squadron aircraft operating over France, dropping a total of 210 containers, fourteen panniers and twenty-four SAS troops. Successful.

——11/12.09.44

SOE Operation 'Glover 18'. 2243–0424 hrs.
Stirling IV, EF264 'Z'.
2nd navigator Flt Sgt Stephens.

Supply drop over France. Successful.

——17.09.44

Operation 'Market'. 1033–1553 hrs.
Stirling IV, LK4O5 'W'.
2nd pilot Flt Sgt Backhouse.

Towed Horsa DP283 (Chalk no. 437) to LZ 'Z', six miles west of Arnhem. Horsa flown by Staff Sgt Westell and Sgt Evans. Carried one jeep, one trailer, one heavy machine gun and seven troops. Horsa cast off successfully and seen to land two miles south-west of LZ.

Crossed in Dutch coast:	1257 hrs at position:
	51.43N
	03.43E
	2,500 ft
Over LZ:	1336–1339 hrs
Crossed out Dutch coast:	1413 hrs at position:
	51.43N
	03.43E
	11,000 ft

Two Horsas and one Waco seen in sea at position: 51.58N 02.14E. Boat was seen taking personnel off the Waco, but nobody was seen on the Horsas. At 1320 hrs approx. position 51.38N 04.45E, Horsa seen in the sea. Boats but no troops to be seen. Small amount of flak, but no fighter opposition encountered.

Note: Horsa DP283 was the fifth production Horsa to be built, and at the time of 'Market' was two-and-a-half years old. For much of that time it served with the Heavy Glider Conversion Unit at Brize Norton.

——18.09.44

Operation 'Market'.
Stirling IV – unidentified.

Towed Horsa glider to LZ 'X' (adjoining LZ 'Z'). Successful. Flak opposition much stronger than on previous day.

——20.9.44

Operation 'Market'. 1512–2000 hrs.
Stirling IV – unidentified.

Resupply to DZ 200 yds west of the Hartenstein Hotel at Oosterbeek, west of Arnhem. Dropped twenty-four containers and four panniers. Seventeen squadron aircraft operating. Intense flak. Aircraft damaged in nose section.

——26/27.09.44

SOE Operation. 2307–0448 hrs.
Stirling IV, LJ934 'Y'.

Supply drop over France. Unsuccessful – no reception.

——09/12.10.44

Operation 'Molten'.
Stirling IV – unidentified.

Ferried Horsa glider to Italy, Successful. Glider landed safely at Chiampino (Rome) and Stirling landed at Pomigliano (Naples). Returned to Fairford afternoon of 12 October, carrying repatriated service personnel.

——04.11.44

Sea search, 0644–1227 hrs.
Stirling IV, LK4-05 'W'.

Search for Stirling of 295 Squadron missing from SOE Operation 'Halter 6', in the Eksund area of Norway. Nothing found.

——06/07.11.44

SOE Operation 'Halter 1' (59.20.50N 08.55.00E). 2031–0435 hrs
Stirling IV, LK4O5 'W'.

Supply drop over Norway. Unsuccessful – no reception. Six squadrons operating.

——14/15.01.45

SOE Operation 'Rummy 20' (52.00.53N 04.32.02E). 2001–0022 hrs.
Stirling IV, LJ997 'T'.

Supply drop over Holland. Successful. Twenty-four containers and five packages dropped. Success mainly due to Eureka beacon on DZ. Only successful squadron sortie that night. Five squadron aircraft operating.

——07/08.02.45

Bombing Operation, Kalkar. 2136–0243 hrs.
Stirling IV, LKA05 'W'.

Troop concentrations moving through the town. Bomb load: twenty-one 500 lb MC. Bombs seen to burst in target area. Slight amount of flak, but mostly too far away to be of any concern. Ten squadron aircraft operating.

——22/23.02.45

SOE Operation 'Pommel 6' (60.08.00N 10.34.30E). 1840–0325 hrs.
Stirling IV, EF264 'Z'.

Supply drop over Norway. Unable to find briefed DZ so dropped on 'Pommel-15' (60.09.20N 10.32.16E) instead. At 2320 hrs a single-engined aircraft was seen in the DZ area, but it did not attack the Stirling or the reception committee. At 2344 hrs, in position 59.53N 09.50E, a twin-engined aircraft crossed the Stirling's track at right angles. It turned in and followed for a short time but did not attack. Landed at Kinloss.

Note: A total of fifty-one Stirlings flew SOE operations over Norway this night. German fighters were active, but they were able to claim only one Stirling; this was LK566 of 190 Squadron.

——02/03.04.45

SOE operation 'Crupper 49' (60.10.45N 09.50.23E). 2116–0630 hrs.
Stirling IV, LJ818 'X'.
2nd flight engineer Sgt Bateman.

Supply drop over Norway. Successful. Fifteen containers and three packages dropped. One container hung-up and brought back to base. Inaccurate light flak encountered at position 58.16N 09.36E. Coastal lighthouses difficult to identify.

——07/08.04.45

SAS operation 'Amherst 13' (Assen area). 1951–0056 hrs.
Stirling IV, EE900 'W'.
2nd flight engineer Plt Off Fairweather.

Paratroop operation over Holland. Successful. Dense stratus cloud covered the DZ. With the aid of GEE fixes our fifteen paratroops were dropped 'blind'. Flak and fires seen at Ameland. Eight squadron aircraft operating.

Note: Operation 'Amherst' was a paratroop invasion of north-east Holland, carried out by the 2nd Battalion SAS. Purpose was to capture bridges to aid the 2nd Canadian Division in its drive to clear the area of a large pocket of German resistance.

——14/15.04.45

SOE operation 'Blinkers 2' (60.H.58N 05.44.30E). 2135–0600 hrs.
Stirling IV, EE900 'W'.

Supply drop over Norway. Successful. The pilot considered that too many flame floats were used by the other aircraft. No enemy activity of any kind. Diverted to Langham on return. Six squadron aircraft operating.

Note: The following three operations are not noted in the squadron's Form 541. As a result, details of flight times, aircraft flown etc are unavailable.

——18.04.45

To Brussels, from where liberated POWs were flown to Wing, Bucks. Ten squadron aircraft operating.

——19.04.45

One of ten squadron crews detailed to carry full loads of petrol to B120 Hanover. Each aircraft carried seventeen panniers, each containing seven-and-a-half 4½ gall cans of petrol. Owing to strong crosswinds, Hanover would not accept these aircraft, two of which landed at B226 Wunstorf. The others went to B58 Brussels and unloaded there, after which they and the first two aircraft embarked a total of 292 former POWs and flew them to Wing.

——22.04.45

One of fifteen squadron crews detailed for B50 Vitry-en-Artois to transport ground personnel of 137 Wing (226 and 342 Squadrons) to B77 Gilze-Rijen. There was a delay at B50 as the Wing's Mitchell bombers had not taken off and the ground crews could not be released. Eventually, ten of the Stirlings loaded up and with four of the empty aircraft (the other had gone o/s) went to B77, where there was a further delay. The number of ex-POWs to be taken was less than expected and eventually only seven aircraft were required, six going to Westcott, Bucks and the other to Dunsfold, in Surrey.

——10.05.45

Operation 'Doomsday 1'.
Base – Gardermoen. 0255–0725 hrs.
Gardermoen – Base. 0820–1330 hrs.
Stirling IV, EE900 'W'.

One of twenty-five squadron aircraft carrying elements of the 1st Airborne Division to Norway. Owing to a weather front lying across the North Sea and Norway and covering Gardermoen, only fifteen aircraft landed at the destination airfield.

——12.05.45

Operation 'Doomsday 2'.
Base – Gardermoen. 1035–1335 hrs.
Gardermoen – Base. 1525–1930 hrs.
Stirling IV, PW442 'P'.

Search made en route for two squadron aircraft missing from the previous operation. Nothing found.

——13.05.45

Operation 'Doomsday 3'. Base – Gardermoen. 1139–1525 hrs.

——15.05.45

Gardermoen – Base. 0942-1339 hrs.
Stirling IV, LJ993 'V'.

Two nights at Gardermoen due to bad weather.

Appendix 2

Stirlings Flown by the Isaacson Crew

The sortie tally for each Stirling refers to the sorties flown While that aircraft was on 190 Squadron. Being the second squadron to equip with Stirling IVs, 190 received many of its original aircraft direct from the makers. However, many of its later aircraft had previously flown with other squadrons, one example being EE900. Built as a Mark III, this Stirling flew nine sorties as such with 90 Squadron of Bomber Command, before conversion to Mark IV standard and subsequent allocation to 190 Squadron.

Of the Stirlings noted below, three were lost to enemy action – all of them at Arnhem. A fourth was written off in a take-off crash at Great Dunmow.

A/C	On Unit	Sorties	Remarks
EE900	?	4	To 23 MU May 1945. SOC 05.06.47.
EF242	11.05.44	26	To 23 MU 17.05.45. SOC 05.06.47.
EF264	27.04.44	26	To 23 MU 20.04.45. SOC 14.01.46.
LJ816	21.04.44	17	To 23 MU 11.12.44. SOC 26.12.46.
LJ818	25.01.44	29	To 3 Para Brigade as ground trainer. Re-serialised 5051M.
LJ820	21.01.44	11	To 23 MU (date unknown). SOC 14.11.46
LJ831	26.01.44	24	FTR Arnhem 20.09.44. Crash-landed Ghent airfield with flak damage. Written off.

LJ832	27.01.44	24	To 23 MU 20.04.45. SOC 05.06.47.
LJ881	17.05.44	10	FTR Arnhem 21.09.44.
LJ993	14.06.44	1	To 23 MU 31.05.45. SOC 05.06.47.
LJ934	?.05.44	11	To 23 MU 31.05.45. SOC 05.06.47.
LJ936	21.05.44	12	To 23 MU 31.05.45. SOC 05.06.47.
LJ982	11.06.44	8	FTR Arnhem 27.09.44.
LJ997	?	5	Crashed on take-off, Great Dunmow, for Operation 'Varsity', 24.03.45.
LK405	?	22	To 23 MU April 1945. SOC 07.02.46.
PW442	03.05.45		Operated post-war only. To 23 MU 25.05.45. SOC 05.06.47.

Appendix 3

Airfields Operated From

The following notes relate to the airfields as they were in the period 1944–45. The Ordnance Survey (OS) map references are taken from the Landranger series.

——Fairford, Gloucester

Nine miles north of Swindon, and two miles south of Fairford town.

Position:	51.41N 01.47W
Hardstandings:	Spectacle – 52
OS Ref:	SP 150990 (163)
Hangars:	T2 – 2
Height ASL:	260 ft
Accommodation:	Temporary
Runways:	23/05 – 6,000 x 150 ft 28/10 – 4,200 x 150 ft 33/15 – 4,200 x 150 ft
Obstruction:	Kempsford Church 180°N at 2,300 yds.
Railway station:	Fairford (GWR). Closed 18.06.62.

Airfield currently (2006) operated by United States Air Force.

——Great Dunmow, Essex

Six-and-a-half miles east of Bishops Stortford.

Position:	51.53N
	00.19E
Hardstandings:	Spectacle – 50
OS Ref:	TF 592235 (167)
Hangars:	T2 – 2
	Blister – 1
Height ASL:	325 ft
Accommodation:	Temporary
Runways:	33/15 – 6,000 x 150 ft
	29/11 – 4,200 x 150 ft
	22/05 – 4,200 x 150 ft
Landmark (day):	Easton Lodge
	023° N at 300 yards
	This was built as a private station for the inhabitants of Easton Lodge. It became a public station in September 1895.

Airfield sold for agricultural use in April 1958.

——Tarrant Rushton, Dorset

Four miles east of Blandford.

Position:	50.51N 02.04W
Hardstandings:	Spectacle – 50
OS Ref:	ST 946058 (195)
Hangars:	T2 – 2
Height ASL:	255 ft
Accommodation:	Temporary
Runways:	01/19 – 6,000 x 150 ft 08/26 – 4,200 x 150 ft 13/31 – 4,200 x 150 ft
Landmark (day):	Tumuli (Badbury Rings), 140°N, at 1½ miles.
Railway station:	Blandford (LMS)

Airfield closed for all flying 26.01.81.

Appendix 4

Operation 'Market': 190 Squadron

	P/TROOPS		G.TOWING		RESUPPLY		LOAD LIFTED	FTR	KIA	POW	RET
	DES	SUC	DES	SUC	DES	SUC					
17.09	6	6	-	-	-	-	97 pathfinder paratroops	-	-	-	-
	-	-	19	18	-	-	130 troops, 17 jeeps, 1 light/1 heavy motorcycle	-	-	-	-
18.09	-	-	21	17	-	-	92 troops, 19 jeeps, 21 trailers, 7x5 cwt cars, 4x6 pdr guns, 1 heavy motorcycle	-	-	-	-
19.09	-	-	2	1	-	-	6 troops, 2 jeeps, 3 trailers	-	-	-	-

	-	-	-	-	16	14	384 containers, 64 panniers	2	8	2	3
20.09	-	-	-	-	17	-14	408 containers, 68 panniers	3	6	2	11
21.09	-	-	-	-	10	3	240 containers, 40 panniers	7	24	8	14
23.09	-	-	-	-	7	7	168 containers, 28 panniers	-	-	-	-
Totals:	6	6	42	36	50	42	N/A	12	38	12	28

Appendix 5

190 Squadron: Genesis

No. 190 Squadron was first formed at Newmarket on 24 October 1917. The role was to provide basic training in night flying, for which it operated BE2 variants and Airco DH6s supplemented, in January 1918, by Avro 504s. At some time in 1918 the squadron moved to Upwood, where it was disbanded in January 1919.

No. 190 Squadron reformed on March 1943 at Sullom Voe as a unit of 18 Group, Coastal Command. Equipped with Catalina lb's, the squadron was tasked with anti-submarine patrols over the North Atlantic and the Norwegian Sea. Flights of more than twenty hours were not uncommon.

The first operation was flown on 7 March. This was an uneventful crossover patrol to the north east on Iceland, the total flight time being 21 hours 30 min.

The first action came on 26 March. P/O Fish was making an ice patrol when he sighted and attacked a fully surfaced submarine near Jan Mayen Island. The U-boat (U-339) at first fought back and then dived, but was badly damaged by depth charges, forcing it to cut short its patrol and return to Trondheim for repairs. The Catalina was hit by return fire, but the damage was slight and none of the crew was hurt. It continued its patrol and shortly afterwards sighted a second U-boat, which promptly crash-dived.

A rescue operation was carried out on 14 June, when S/L J A Holmes alighted in the North Atlantic to pick up eight downed airmen. They were the survivors of a Fortress of 206 Squadron which had ditched north west of the Faroes three days earlier.

U-Boats were not the only enemies encountered. On 7 July F/O J Fish (again) engaged a Blohm and Voss BV 138 three engined flying boat, a type rarely seen by allied airmen. The German machine was driven of, with one engine smoking and the rear turret out of action.

On 1 January 1944, the squadron suffered a paper disbandment, when it was re-numbered 210 Squadron.

The squadron did not remain in limbo for long. On 5 January 1944, Air Ministry signal 02483 authorised the formation of 190 Squadron in 38 Group, AEAF. The squadron was to form at Leicester East with an establishment of sixteen planes plus four reserve Stirlings.

——15/18.01.44

F/O Anderson, F/O Le Bouvier and their crews reported from 1665 OCU, Tilstock. As there were no duties for them to perform they were immediately sent on seven-day leave.

——20.01.44

F/O Duveen, from 84 Group, reported for duty as adjutant. The squadron's first two Stirlings, LJ823 and LJ827, arrived from Short Bros, Belfast.

——21.01.44

F/L Gardiner and crew arrived on posting from 1665 OCU and proceeded on seven-day leave. Stirlings LJ816, LJ820, LJ822, LK431 and EF270 arrived from Short Bros, Belfast.

——22.01.44

F/O Stewart reported for duty as Radar Officer. Stirlings LJ825, LJ82 and LJ831 arrived from Short Bros, Belfast.

——23.01.44

W/C Harrison arrived from Tilstock for an inspection, and returned there that night.

——24.01.44

F/L Harmay reported for duty as Engineering Officer.

——20/24.01.44

During this period very little could be done, except for inspection of Technical and Domestic sites and checking of furniture – no ground crews having been posted in, with the exception of F/S Knapp, W/O Mech.

——25.01.44

W/O Harrison arrived from Tilstock to take over as Commanding Officer. Buildings on the technical site were taken over. Stirlings LJ818, LJ828 and EF214 were delivered.

——26.01.44

All aircrew on leave returned for duty. Flight and admin offices were opened up and furnished. W/C Harrison visited HQ 38 Group regarding personnel and other matters.

——29.01.44

Stirling LJ830 delivered.

——30.01.44

One sergeant, two corporals and eighteen airmen attached from 32 MU St Athan to carry out mods to squadron aircraft.

——31.04.44

The first ground personnel reported for duty on posting to the squadron. No flying was carried out during the month of January.

——01.02.44

Ground personnel reported for duty.

——02.02.44

Ground personnel reported for duty.

——03.02.44

Ground personnel reported for duty. Stirling LJ833 delivered.

——04.02.44

Ground personnel reported for duty.

——05.02.44

F/O Siegert and crew reported for duty.

——07.02.44

F/L Davison reported for duty as Gunnery Leader.

——08.02.44

F/O Pasco, F/S Herger, F/S Brain, F S Croudis, F/S Middleton and their crews reported for duty. Capt Ellis, Airborne Division, reported for duty as Liason Officer.

——09.02.44

F/O Chesterton reported for duty.

——10.02.44

F/O Selby reported for duty as Electrical Officer. Stirling EF260 delivered. Conference at SHQ to discuss centralised maintenance.

Attending were the COs and Engineering Officers of 190 and 620 Squadrons, and the CTOs of 38 Group and A.D.G.B.

——13.02.44

S/L Gilliard DFC reported from Defford for duty as Flight Commander. Sgt Porter and crew reported for duty.

——19.02.44

Capt Priest, Lt Telfer and 22 NCOs, Glider Pilot Regiment, attached for duty with the squadron.

——21.02.44

F/O Kilgour, F/S Brierly, F/S McMillan and their crews reported for duty.

——23.02.44

W/C Harrison, F/L Davison and Capt Ellis flew to Ringway to arrange a short parachute course for Air Bombers. However, no such course could be arranged.

——25.02.44

F/O Beberfield, Sgt Ellis and their crews reported for duty.

——26.02.44

W/C Harrison proceeded to HQ 38 Group and RAF Fairford to discuss the forthcoming squadron move.

——01.03.44

W/C Harrison flew Stirling LJ 833 on a local air test and also for testing of special equipment. This was the first flight by an aircraft of the squadron, the crew being W/C Harrison, F/L Davidson,

P/O Stewart, F/O Prowse, Sgt Jones, Sgt Thomson and Sgt Alderson. F/L Chappell and crew reported for duty.

——02.03.44

F/O Pasco and crew flew a practise flight, the route being: Market Rasen, Downham Market, Maidenhead and base. Flight time 2 hrs 10 mins. P/O Port, F/S Derbyshire and their crews reported for duty.

——03.03.44

S/L Gilliard and crew flew a practise flight of 1 hr 10 mins. Later the same day F/O Chesterton flew across country. F/L Cottingham, F/S Jones and their crews reported for duty. F/O Pattinson reported for duty. F/L Skinner reported for duty as Signals Leader. F/L Merchant reported for duty as Bombing Leader.

——06.03.44

F/S Sellars, F/S Sutherland and their crews reported for duty.

——07.03.44

The first glider-towing sorties were flown by S/L Gilliard (LJ824) and F/L Gardiner (LK431).

Note: from now on, glider-towing sorties were flown with increasing frequency.

——22.03.44

To prepare for the squadron move to Fairford, an advance party consisting of F/O Adamson, W/O Marsh and six airmen were flown to Fairford by F/O Hay.

——23.03.44

A further advance party consisting of F/L Merchant and 36 airmen proceeded to Fairford by rail.

——25.03.44

The main party, consisting of an air party towing fully laden gliders, and a rail party, proceeded to Fairford. F/O Duveen and F/O Cooke were in charge of the rail party, which left at 12.30 hrs and arrived at Fairford at 19.00 hrs. The air party, consisting of 'A' and 'B' Flights, proceeded at intervals and arrived without incident. Squadron personnel at this time comprised:

55 officers

80 glider pilots

133 NCOs (aircrew)

6 Naval petty officers

27 NCOs (ground crew)

147 Naval ratings

276 airmen

5 NCOs detached from HGMU

17 WAAF

33 airmen

——27.03.44

Flying resumed after the squadron move. Five cross-country glider-tows were flown, three of them being low-level at 500 ft.

——29.03.44

F/L Gardiner and F/O Anderson were detailed to proceed to Tarrant Rushton for a special operation, which was later cancelled.

——31.12–03.01.44

F/L Gardiner and F/O Anderson, operating from Tarrant Rushton, flew an SOE operation over France, Unsuccessful. No reception.

——02.04.44

S/L Gilliard's crew (F/O Lawton, P/O Redding, P/O McEwan, Sgt Towers and Sgt Byrne) reported for duty.

——03.04.44

Sgt Isaacson and crew reported for duty.

——05/06.04.44

Operating from Tarrant Rushton, F/O Hay, F/O Pasco and F/S Brain flew an SOE operation over France. Unsuccessful, no reception.

——08.04.44

F/O Connell and crew reported for duty.

——11/12.04.44

Operating from Tarrant Rushton, six aircraft were detailed for SOE operations over France. F/S Croudis crashed soon after take-off (at Hampreston near Bournemouth) with no survivors. F/O Chesterton and F/O Matheson successfully dropped their loads on the DZ. The other three crews saw no reception signals and were forced to bring back their loads.

——18.04.44

Sgt Coeshot and crew reported for duty.

——19.04.44

F/S Fogarty and crew reported for duty.

Appendix 6

SOE/SAS Drop Zones Noted

<table>
<tr><td>Amherst 13</td><td>Holland</td><td>SAS</td><td colspan="2">Map ref: v160937</td></tr>
<tr><td>Blinkers 2</td><td>Norway</td><td>SOE</td><td>60.11.58N</td><td>05.44.30E</td></tr>
<tr><td>Crop 25</td><td>Norway</td><td>SOE</td><td>60.11.15N</td><td>10.49.30E</td></tr>
<tr><td>Crupper 49</td><td>Norway</td><td>SOE</td><td>60.10.45N</td><td>09.50.23E</td></tr>
<tr><td>Donald</td><td>France</td><td>SOE</td><td></td><td></td></tr>
<tr><td>Dudley 3</td><td>Holland</td><td>SOE</td><td>52.42.24N</td><td>05.42.10E</td></tr>
<tr><td>Francis</td><td>France</td><td>SAS</td><td></td><td></td></tr>
<tr><td>Gain 20</td><td>France</td><td>SAS</td><td></td><td></td></tr>
<tr><td>Glover 18</td><td>France</td><td>SOE</td><td>48.01.55N</td><td>05.45.18E</td></tr>
<tr><td>Grog</td><td>France</td><td>SAS</td><td></td><td></td></tr>
<tr><td>Halter 1</td><td>Norway</td><td>SOE</td><td>59.20.50N</td><td>08.55.00E</td></tr>
</table>

Halter 6	Norway	SOE		
Pommel 6	Norway	SOE	60.08.00N	10.34.30E
Pommel 15	Norway	SOE	60.09.20N	10.32.16E
Rummy 20	Holland	SOE	52.00.53N	04.32.02E
Stationer 174	France	SOE		
Stirrup	Norway	SOE	60.25.00N	09.07.00E
Town Hall 8	France	SOE		

Appendix 7

Aircrew State, 190 Squadron Operation 'Market'

The following lists the aircrew involved during the period of Operation 'Market'. Crew changes and additions for the same period are also noted.

Pilot:	W/C G E Harrison DFC
Nav:	W/O D Mathewson
A/B:	F/O N Mackay
W/Op:	F/L N E Skinner
F/E:	Sgt R Percy
A/G:	W/O J F B De Cordove
21/09 – 2nd pilot:	W/O Brierly

Pilot:	S/L J P Gilliard DFC
Nav:	F/O R Lawton
A/B:	F/O R Cullen
W/Op:	F/S H Towers
F/E:	F/S C T Byrne
A/G:	F/O N S McEwan
19/09 – W/Op:	C H Lane

Pilot:	S/L D S Gibb
Nav:	F/O J Fargher
A/B:	F/O P Cordy
W/Op:	P/O M Booth
F/E:	P/O K Shepherd

A/G:	Sgt T A R Rogerson
Pilot:	F/L A Anderson
Nav:	P/O J H Adamson
A/B:	F/O G E Orange
W/Op:	F/S W G Tolley
F/E:	Sgt R J Smith
A/G:	Sgt A G Bellamy
18/09 – 2nd Pilot:	F/L Merchant
19/09 – 2nd Pilot:	F/S Cory-Chandler
21/09 – 2nd Pilot:	F/S/ Cory-Chandler
Pilot:	F/L O C C Bliss
Nav:	W/O K C March
A/B:	F/S C H Cockerill
W/Op:	Sgt D E Hanson
F/E:	Sgt G W Fairweather
A/G:	Sgt J F Missaubie
Pilot:	F/L W G Gardiner
Nav:	F/S J G Williams
A/B:	F/S G R Douglas
W/Op:	F/S G E Ames
F/E:	Sgt R A Cramp
A/G:	Sgt J F Coghlan
19/09 – 2nd Pilot:	W/O G P Wylie
21/09 – W/Op:	W/O A J Collins
21/09 – A/G:	F/L R G Davidson
Pilot:	F/L D R Robertson
Nav:	F/O L E Prowse
A/B:	F/L N L Roseblade
W/Op:	F/S G E Thompson

F/E:	F/S S R Alderson
A/G:	F/S A G Davies
19/09 A/G:	Sgt G Hopkins
19/09 2nd A/G:	Sgt L G Haldock

Pilot:	F/O H B Allen
Nav:	F/O W C Summers
A/B:	F/S G T Cunningham
W/Op:	Sgt J F Bradbrook
F/E:	Sgt K Kendrew
A/G:	F/S C P Randall

Pilot:	F/O G H Chesterton
Nav:	F/S H J Whitting
A/B:	F/S D W Smith
W/Op:	W/O J Knighton
F/E:	Sgt J Macready
A/G:	F/S R G Shaw

Pilot:	F/O S J Connell
Nav:	F/O E B Reynolds
A/B:	F/S F West
W/Op:	W/O L Dowling
F/E:	Sgt A Ell
A/G:	W/O K A Conley
18/09 – 2nd Pilot:	P/O Arthy

Pilot:	F/O A C Farren
Nav:	F/S F Ross
A/B:	F/S W L P Cairns
W/Op:	F/S W Skewes
F/E:	F/S P Stone
A/G:	F/S A J H Brown

19/09 2nd Pilot:	Sgt Redfern
21/09 2nd A/B:	W/O L J Billen

Pilot:	F/O/ J S Hay
Nav:	F/S K G Y Newcombe
A/B:	F/S C I Duncan
W/Op:	F/O J R Clague
F/E:	Sgt J J Lowe
A/G:	F/S A G West
18/09 – 2nd Pilot:	F/O Cullen
21/09 – Nav:	F/S C I Duncan
21/09 – A/B:	F/S J F Povey

Pilot:	F/O J C Le Bouvier
Nav:	W/O D Mathewson
A/B:	F/S D Martin
W/Op:	F/S S F Sanders
F/E:	Sgt C Ryan
A/G:	F/S C Kershaw
18/09 – 2nd Pilot:	F/S Wimms
19/09 – 2nd Pilot:	F/S Wimms
19/09 – Nav:	F/O T Oliver

Appendix 8

Commanding Officers: 190 Squadron

Unknown	24.10.17	
	?.01.19	Squadron disbanded
W/C P H Allington DFC	01.03.43	Posted in from 210 Squadron
	01.01.44	Squadron disbanded
W/C G E Harrison DFC	05.01.44	Posted in from 1665 HCU
	21.09.44	Killed in action
W/C R H Bunker DSO DFC & Bar	04.10.44	Posted in from 620 Squadron
	20.04.45	Killed in flying accident
W/C G H Briggs DFC	24.04.45	Posted in from School of Air Support
	25.06.45	Posted out to 620 Squadron
W/C Bartram	25.06.45	Posted in from ORTU
	21.01.46	Squadron disbanded

Appendix 9

Squadron Bases

Newmarket, Suffolk	24.10.17	Squadron formed. Moved to Upwood.
Upwood, Hants	1919	
	1919	Squadron disbanded. Reformed at Sullom Voe
Sullom Voe, Shetland	01.03.43	Detachments at Reykjavik and Castle Archdale.
	01.01.44	Squadron disbanded. Reformed at Leicester East.
Leicester East, Leicester	01.01.44	
Fairford, Gloucester	25.03.44	
Great Dunmow, Essex	14.10.44	
Tarrant Rushton, Dorset	05.11.45	
	25.01.46	Squadron disbanded.

Appendix 10

30 Group: Operations and Losses

20 SEPTEMBER 1944

The Group's effort for this day (an all-Stirling affair) was divided into two parts, the first of which called for 33 Stirlings of No's 196 and 299 Sqdns to drop supplies on LZ E1. Taking off later, the second part of the operation called for 67 Stirlings of No's 190, 295, 570 and 620 squadrons, together with 64 Dakotas of 46 Group, to drop supplies on a drop zone one mile SSE of LZ V.

With slight amendments the southern route was chosen, in order that the aircraft could take advantage of the Allied-held Eindhoven-Nijmegen corridor. The route was Bases-Hatfield-Bradwell-Ostend-Herenthals-Veghel-Drop Zone, returning on reciprocal.

Aircraft were to fly at 2500 ft outbound, in loose pairs, descend to 1000 ft for the drop, then return at 4000 ft. In the event, at least one squadron (No. 570) flew in loose lines astern, at one point as high as 6,000 ft. Of the 100 Stirlings dispatched, ninety claimed successful drops. Intense flak was encountered over both drop zones, and eleven Stirlings failed to return, with many others being damaged.

Note: the Isaacson crew took off at 2512 hrs and landed at 2000 hrs.

Losses

LZ 'Z' – 190 Squadron

——LJ840

F/S J P Averill.
Took off approx 1200 hrs.

Hit by flak over DZ and set on fire. Crew all baled out safely.

——LJ851

W/O G R Oliver.
Took off approx 1200 hrs.

Shot down before reaching DZ. Crashed south of Eindhoven. Crew safe.

——LJ947

P/O W L Marshall.
Took off approx 1200 hrs.

Crash-landed at Alost, Belgium, with flak damage to port engines. Crew safe. Aircraft damaged beyond repair.

——LJ954

P/O J F Ellis.
Took off approx 1205 hrs.

Crash landed north of Brussels with flak damage. Pilot injured.

——LJ998

W/O W R Tait
Took off approx 1430 hrs.

No survivors.

——LK556

F/O J W McOmie
Took off 1205 hrs.

Crashed near Elst approx 1430 hrs with flak damage. Sgt D N Clough (F/E) killed, as were two army dispatchers. Remainder of crew evaded and returned to Allied lines.

Drop Zone 691785 (one mile SSE of LZ 'L') – 190 Squadron

——LJ829

F/O R J Matheson.
Took off 1502 hrs.

Believed shot down by flak. Crashed at Doorwerth with no survivors.

Pilot:	F/O R J Matheson
Nav:	F/O R A Davis
A/B:	F/S K Willet
Disp:	L/Cpl Rextrew
W/OP:	W/O T K Allen
F/E	Sgt E F Keen
A/G:	W/O D L Brouse
Disp:	Drv J F Leech

——LJ831

F/L D R Robertson.
Took off 1508 hrs.

Hit by flat over D/Z. Aircraft went into steep dive with damaged elevator trim tabs. With the aid of the A/B, control was regained and belly-landing eventually made on Ghent airfield. No casualties. All returned to unit.

Pilot:	F/L D R Robertson
Nav:	F/O L E Prowse
A/B:	F/L N L Roseblade
W/OP:	F/S G E Thompson
F/E:	F/S R Alderson
A/G:	Sgt G Hopkins

——EF831

F/O J O Le Bouvier
Took off 1510 hrs.

Hit by flak and port wing caught fire while on run up to DZ. Crew baled out. Aircraft crashed Arnhem area.

Pilot:	F/O J O Le Bouvier	Evaded
Nav:	W/O A Mathewson	Evaded
A/B:	F/S D Martin	POW
W/Op:	F/S S F Sanders	Evaded
F/E:	Sgt C Ryan	POW
A/G:	F/S C Kershaw	POW
Disp:	Unknown	POW

Appendix 11

Honours and Awards

21.01.44	DFC	W/C G R Harrison, American Silver Star
21.11.44	DFC	W/C R H Bunker, DFC & Bar
	DFC	F/L D R Robertson, French C de G
	DFC	F/O C L Siegert
	DFC	F/O F E Pascoe
	DFC	F/O N W Sutherland
28.11.44	DFM	F/S G E Thompson
	DFM	F/S J S Welton
01.03.45	DFC	F/L N L Roseblade
	American DFC	F/L J O Le Bouvier
	Dutch Bronze Lion	F/L R G Cullen
	Dutch Bronze Cross	F.O D S Sellars

Note: W/C Harrison was awarded the DFC for his 'high skill, fortitude and gallantry' when commanding 149 Squadron in 1943. W/C Bunker was awarded the DSO for his part in Operation 'Market' when he was a flight commander on 620 Squadron.

Appendix 12

190 Squadron
Casualties: Aircraft/Personnel
April 1944–May 1945

——11.04.44 LJ822

SOE operation. Crashed soon after take-off from Tarrant Rushton. Dived into the ground at Knighton Farm, Hampreston, Dorset.

Pilot:	F/S P Croudis (NZ)	Killed
Nav:	F/S D L Sampson (NZ)	Killed
A/B:	F/S L E Zierrach (AUS)	Killed
W/Op:	F/S K S Nunn (AUS)	Killed
F/E:	Sgt J W Mitchell (RAF)	Killed
A/G:	F/O R S Hadley (Can)	Killed

——22.23.07.44 LJ882

SAS operation 'Francis', France. Paratroopers carried. Crashed at Graffigny-Chemin.

Pilot:	F/O L A Kilgour (NZ)	Killed
Nav:	F/O P Vinet (Can)	POW Stalag Luft 4
A/B:	Sgt H L Guy (RAF)	Killed
W/Op:	F/O R G Foy (Can)	Killed
F/E:	Sgt A W Swindell (RAF)	Killed
A/G:	F/S A P Bell (Can)	Evaded

——25.26.08.44 LJ827 'S'

Supply drop over France. Crashed at Villebougis.

Pilot:	F/O N H Port (AUS)	Killed
Nav:	P/O C M Rosay (RAF)	Killed
A/B:	F/S R G Fulcher (RAF)	Injured; returned to UK
W/Op:	F/S K C Garner (RAF)	Killed
F/E:	P/O F C Newman (RAF)	Killed
A/G:	F/S E T Cornelius (RAF)	Evaded
2nd F/E:	Sgt W T Bussell (RAF)	Killed; trainee from 1665 HCU

——19.09.44 LJ939 'A'

Resupply, Operation 'Market'. Shot down by flak and crashed near Oosterbeek.

Pilot:	S/L J P Gilliard DFC (RAF)	Killed
Nav:	F/O R Lawton (RAF)	Evaded
A/B:	F/O R C Cullen	Evaded
W/Op:	P/O C H Lane (RAF)	POW
F/E:	F/S C T Byrne (RAF)	Killed
A/G:	F/O N S McEwan	Killed
Pass:	S/L F N Royle-Bantoft (RAF)	Evaded Staff Officer, 38 Group

——19.09.44 EF263

Resupply, Operation 'Market'. Shot down by flak and crashed at Michielsgestel, Holland.

Pilot:	W/O S H Coeshot (RAF)	Killed
Nav:	F/S S V Davis (RAF)	Killed
A/B:	F/S J G Jeffrey (RAF)	Killed
W/Op:	F/S W C Moss (RAF)	Killed
F/E:	Sgt G L Wood (RAF)	Killed
A/G:	F/S G S Breckles (Can)	Killed

——20.09.44 EF260 'O'

Resupply, Operation 'Market'. Shot down by flak and crashed at Arnhem.

Pilot:	F/O J O Le Bouvier (Can)	Evaded
Nav:	F/O T Oliver (RAF)	Evaded
A/B:	F/S D Martin (RAF)	POW Stalag Luft 7
W/Op:	F/S S F Sanders (RAF)	Evaded
F/E:	F/S C Ryan (RAF)	POW
A/G:	F/S C Kershaw (RAF)	POW Stalag Luft 7
Pass:	Mr Townsend *Daily Telegraph* correspondent	Evaded

——20.09.44 LJ831

Resupply, Operation 'Market'. Hit by flak over DZ. Belly-landed on Ghent airfield, which was in British hands. Aircraft written off.

Pilot:	F/L DR Robertson (Can)	Returned to unit
Nav:	F/O L E Prowse (Can)	Returned to unit
A/B:	F/L N L Roseblade (Can)	Returned to unit
W/Op:	F/S G E Thompson (RAF)	Returned to unit
F/E:	F/S S R Alderson (RAF)	Returned to unit
A/G:	F/S A G Davies (RAF)	Returned to unit

——20.09.44 LJ829

Resupply, Operation 'Market'. Show down by flak and crashed at Doorwerth.

Pilot:	F/O R J Matheson	Killed
Nav:	P/O R A Davis (Aus)	Killed
A/B:	F/S S K Willet (Aus)	Killed
W/Op:	W/O T W Allen (Can)	Killed
F/E:	Sgt E E Keen (RAF)	Killed
A/G:	W/O D L Brouse (Can)	Killed

——21.09.44 LJ982 'N'

Resupply, Operation 'Market'. Shot down by flak and crashed at Zettin.

Pilot:	W/C G E Harrison DFC (RAF)	Killed
Nav:	W/O D Mathewson (NZ)	Killed
A/B:	F/O N Mackey (RAF)	Killed
W/Op:	F/L N E Skinner (RAF)	Killed
F/E:	Sgt R Percy (RAF)	Evaded; died of injuries
A/G:	W/O J F B de Cordove (Can)	Killed
2nd Pilot:	W/O Brierly	Killed

——21.09.44 LJ833

Resupply, Operation 'Market'. Shot down by flak and fighters. Ditched in River Maas near Demen and broke up.

Pilot:	F/L A Anderson (RAF)	Killed
Nav:	P/O J H Adamson (RAF)	Killed
A/B:	F/O G E Orange (RAF)	Killed
W/Op:	F/S W G Tolley (RAF)	Killed
F/E:	Sgt A J Smith (RAF)	Killed
A/G:	Sgt A G Bellamy (RAF)	Killed
2nd Pilot:	F/S Cory-Chandler	Killed

——21.09.44 LJ881

Resupply, Operation 'Market'. Shot down by flak and fighters and crashed at Herveld.

Pilot:	F/O B A Beberfald (NZ)	Killed
Nav:	W/O N J Yarwood (NZ)	Killed
A/B:	F/S G A Phillips (Aus)	Killed
W/Op:	F/L L N Munro (Can)	Killed
F/E:	Sgt C F Branson (RAF)	Killed
A/G:	W/O G Morris (Aus)	Evaded

——21.09.44 LJ943

Resupply, Operation 'Market'. Shot down by flak and crashed at Zettin.

Pilot:	P/O R B Herger (Can)	Killed
Nav:	F/O O H Antoft (Can)	Killed
A/B:	F/O J K MacDonnel (Can)	Killed
W/Op:	F/S L I Whitlock (Can)	Killed

F/E:	Sgt L G Hilliard (RAF)	POW, wounded Stalag Luft 7
A/G:	W/O J G Thomas (Can)	POW, wounded
2nd Nav:	F/O H A Thornington	Killed

——21.09.44 LJ823

Resupply, Operation 'Market'. Hit over DZ by flak, then attacked by fighters. Crash-landed at Wijchen.

Pilot:	F/O A C Farren (RAF)	Injured (after baling out)
Nav:	F/S F Ross (RAF)	Baled out, returned to unit
A/B:	F/S W L P Cairns	Killed, baled out too low
W/Op:	F/S W Skewes (RAF)	Killed, baled out too low
F/E:	F/S P Stone (RAF)	Injured (after baling out)
A/G:	F/S A J H Brown (RAF)	Injured (after baling out)
2ns A/B:	W/O L J Billen	Killed, baled out too low

——21.09.44 LJ916

Resupply, Operation 'Market'. Crashed at Tilburg.

Pilot:	F/O J S Hay (RAF)	POW Stalag Luft 1
Nav:	F/S C I Duncan (RAF)	POW Stalag Luft 7
A/B:	F/S J F Povey (RAF)	POW Stalag Luft 7
W/Op:	F/O J R Clague (RAF)	POW Stalag Luft 3
F/E:	Sgt J J Lowe (RAF)	POW Stalag Luft 7
A/G:	F/S A G West (RAF)	POW Stalag 357

——20.04.45 LJ930 'A'

SOE operation to Norway ('Blinkers 2'). Cause of loss and crash site unknown.

Pilot:	F/O A J Lewis (RAF)	Killed
Nav:	F/O R Weldon (RAF)	Killed
A/B:	F/S A P Hillier (RAF)	Killed
W/Op:	F/S J G Cartmell (RAF)	Killed
F/E:	Sgt H V Barrow (RAF)	Killed
A/G:	F/S W H Ogilvie (RAF)	Evaded
2nd Nav:	F/S T W Booker (RAF)	Killed

——20.04.45 LJ930 'A'

Ferried petrol supplies to Brussels and returned with liberated ex-POWs, landing at Odiham. Took off from Odiham with a flat tail wheel and soon after the tail caught fire. Aircraft crashed at Woodlands Lane, Windlesham, Surrey.

Pilot:	W/C R H Bunker DSO DFC (RAF)	Killed
Nav:	Sgt F C King (RAF)	Killed
A/B:	F/O G R T Taylor	Killed
W/Op:	P/O S A Sulsh (RAF)	Killed
F/E:	Sgt R L Bagley	Killed
A/G:	Sgt J Aldred	Killed

——03.05.45 LK196 'B'

Swung on take off for exercise 'amber' and undercarriage collapsed. Aircraft written off. Crew unhurt.

——10.05.45 LJ899

Operation 'Doomsday', air-lifting elements of 1st Airborne Division to Norway. The aircraft went out of control after fabric was seen flapping on the port wing. Ditched in Rydafors Lake, Sweden. No serious injuries to the crew, but four of the passengers were killed.

Pilot:	F/O E Atkinson (RAF)	Returned to unit
Nav:	Sgt K H Rundle (RAF)	Returned to unit
A/B:	F/O W S Long	Returned to unit
W/Op:	F/O H Ashton (RAF)	Returned to unit
F/E:	Sgt W Wright (RAF)	Returned to unit
A/G:	Sgt W Flynn (RAF)	Returned to unit

——10.05.45 LK297

Operation 'Doomsday'. Crashed ten miles north of Oslo as a result, it is believed, of loss of control in bad visibility.

Pilot:	S/L D R Robertson (Can) DFC	Killed
Nav:	F/L R E Prowse (Can)	Killed
A/B:	F/L N L Roseblade (Can)	Killed
W/Op:	F/S G E Thompson (RAF) DFM	Killed
F/E:	F/S R Alderson (RAF)	Killed
A/G:	F/S A G Davies (RAF)	Killed
2nd Pilot:	AVM J R Scarlet-Streatfield	Killed

Note: AVM Scarlet-Streatfield was AOC of 38 Group.

——11.05.45 Wellington X111 NC489

The undermentioned crew took part in 'Doomsday 1' of the previous day. Due to bad weather they were unable to land at their destination in Gardemoen, and were forced to turn back. Engine trouble prompted a diversion to Eindhoven. They were offered passage in a Wellington of 69 Squadron returning to England, but this crashed on take off from Melsbroek.

Pilot:	F/O E F Insley (Can)	Injured
Nav:	F/O H Vanular (Can)	Killed
A/B:	F/S L C Sharpe (RAF)	Killed
W/Op:	W/O J H Hay (Can)	Killed
F/E:	F/S W Dexter (RAF)	Killed
A/G:	F/S J F Coghlan (RAF)	Evaded

Printed in the United Kingdom
by Lightning Source UK Ltd.
135891UK00001BA/34-48/P